C000000378

ROOSTER

JOHN C. FOSTER

GREY MATTER
P R E S S

CHICAGO

"With *The Isle*, John C. Foster makes a twenty-first century contribution to the tradition of the New England Gothic. Fast-moving, gripping, it's a tale straight from Old Man Atlantic's barnacled treasure chest."

— **John Langan, Bram Stoker Award-winning author of *The Fisherman***

"*Mister White* is a potent and hypnotic brew that blends horror, espionage and mystery. Foster has written the kind of book that keeps the genre fresh and alive and will make fans cheer."

— **Ray Garton, Grand Master of Horror Award winner and Bram Stoker Award-nominated author of *Live Girls* and *Scissors***

"[In Foster's *Dead Men*] the darkness swims across the page, but it is not without light, not without hope. Tense, violent, and sprinkled with humor, it's a gripping read."

— **Richard Thomas, author of *Disintegration***

"Brooding and claustro-phobic, one hell of a scary ride. You won't soon forget your visit to *The Isle*."

PRAISE FOR THE WORK

— **Tom Deady, Bram Stoker Award-winning author of *Haven***

"Foster's *Mister White* is a lightning-paced, globetrotting mashup of espionage, adventure and truly disturbing occult horror. Fun and nasty in all the right places."

— **Paul Tremblay, Bram Stoker Award-winning author of *Survivor Song* and *A Head Full of Ghosts***

"The narrative of [*Night Roads*] is bloody, extremely violent, and downright creepy. Foster's style leans more to atmosphere and setting than deep characterization and instrospection, which suits this kind of horror/action/noir."

— **This is Horror**

"*Mister White* is like Stephen King's *The Stand* meets Ian Fleming's James Bond with Graham Masterton's *The Manitou* thrown in for good measure. It's frenetically paced, spectacularly gory and eerie as hell. Highly recommended!"

— **John F.D. Taff, Bram Stoker Award-nominated author of *The Fearing* and *Little Black Spots***

"With *Dead Men*, Foster has crafted an utterly terrifying road trip from Hell. I haven't been this impressed with an authorial debut since Barker's *Books of Blood*. Foster really is that good. He reads like someone who knows where you live and isn't afraid to kick down your door."

— **Joe McKinney, Bram Stoker Award-winning author of *Dead City* and *The Dead Won't Die***

"The most thrilling thing about Foster's sweeping thriller *Mister White* is how well it's written. If the idea is to put powerful words to paper, then Foster does it. And if the idea is to then use those words to pulley-up walls around a willing reader, trapping them in the world of *Mister White*, Foster does that, too."

— **Josh Malerman, Bram Stoker Award-winning author of** *Bird Box*

"Dripping with claustrophobic malice, crawling with dread and otherness, *The Isle* is a journey into places best left alone. A chilling, disturbing, compelling tale."

— **Alan Baxter, Australian Shadows Award-winning author of** *Served Cold* **and** *Manifest Recall*

"Foster's *Baby Powder and Other Terrifying Subtances* is a swaggering collection. Relentless, smart, gorgeously written, and brimming with black humor. This is a standout collection and a welcome counterpoint to quite horror. It's a stunner."

— **Matthew M. Bartlett, author of** *Creeping Waves*

OF JOHN C. FOSTER

"Imagine a marriage of Barker and Tarantino and you have some inkling of what the dark, gory and often quirky [*Night Roads*] is like."

— **Shotgun Logic**

"If you're the kind of person who seeks out hidden places with awful histories, then *The Isle* is the book is for you. You'll feel the damp and the chill, you'll hear the shrieks and the inhuman mutter, you'll see those children and their awful games. Read it in a safe place."

— **Karen Heuler, author of** *The Inner City*

"Is [*Dead Men*] horror? Is it noir? Is it something in-between? Doesn't matter... Foster crafts lean, mean fiction darker than a serial killer's soul."

— **James Newman, author of** *Ugly as Sin*

"Foster's *Mister White* is a finely tuned cat-and-mouse thriller that reads like a seamless integration of classic John Le Carré-style spy thriller with the best of the Splatterpunk movement. With a stunning ending I'm still reeling from, *Mister White* feels like the same kind of unstoppable force as its titular character."

— **Bracken MacLeod, author of** *Stranded* **and** *Closing Costs*

"Foster masterfully weaves New England folk horror into a hard-boiled murder mystery to form a wholly original and gripping novel that will keep you guessing as the dread builds like a tide rolling over the rocky shore. Strange rituals, hidden histories, and dangerous paranoia intersect on *The Isle* in ways that turn northeastern peculiarity into something uniquely horrific and thoroughly engrossing to read."

— **Ed Kurtz, author of** *The Rib from Which I Remake the World*

This novel remains
the copyright of the author.

No part of this book may be used or reproduced in any
manner whatsoever without written permission of the author
or Grey Matter Press except for brief quotations used for promotion
or in reviews. This novel is a work of fiction. Any reference to
historical events, real people or real locales are used fictitiously.
Other names, characters, places and incidents are products of the
author's imagination, and any resemblance to actual events or
locales or persons, living or dead, is entirely coincidental.

ROOSTER
ISBN-13: 978-1-950569-07-6
Grey Matter Press First Trade Paperback Edition - July 2021

Copyright © 2021 John C. Foster
Cover Design Copyright © 2021 Grey Matter Press
Book Design Copyright © 2021 Grey Matter Press
Edited by Anthony Rivera

All rights reserved

CHICAGO

Grey Matter Press
greymatterpress.com

Grey Matter Press on Facebook
facebook.com/greymatterpress

Dedicated to Alice in Chains

ROOSTER

A NOVEL OF ULTIMATE RETRIBUTION

ONE

- 1 -

It was a shit bar downtown, the kind of place whose personality is no personality unless you know what to look for. The cigarette machine in back still worked and the ladies' room didn't. No juke, but there was a box TV mounted in a corner over the warped mirror. There was no Wi-Fi. There was no top shelf booze, nothing advertised on TV made it onto the shelves, and if you wanted peanuts, there was a bodega on the corner.

HOLIDAY LOUNGE is what the dead sign outside read. The burn-outs inside would rather spend the afternoon nursing a pitcher and a pack of cigarettes than sitting in their subsidized housing. Everyone clinging to the illusion they were among people. If asked—no one ever did—but if any one of them were asked, the whisker-chinned rummies might refer to their pilgrimage here as, "seeing some friends at the Holiday." They weren't friends, but when together they maintained the illusion they weren't alone.

There are places like this all over the country. Between the cracks. Unchanging. All over the world in fact, but I don't use those joints.

I work in the States.

Holiday Lounge is in New York City.

Back when I would talk to my clients, before I understood solitude, I was with a well-dressed man at a dump like the Holiday. Can't remember which city. He was uncomfortable in the place, wiping his jacket sleeve every time it stuck to the table.

"You like French restaurants? Big tits? Hashish? Those are human wants. Human needs. Cracks in your armor."

I remember lighting a cigarette. This version of the Holiday Lounge didn't give two shits about smoking.

"Be a machine. No wants. No needs. Only thinking about survival. Always thinking about survival. Then you might make it."

"What about life? Love?" this fucking family guy said, just paid me with a full briefcase for a corpse.

"Get you killed," I told him, maybe twenty-five years old at the time and already something beyond human.

Already a liar.

- 2 -

I don't dream, never have, but I always wake to the sound of screaming.

Kettle drums were beating a tattoo against the inside of my temples, and my gummy eyes tracked over the ceiling, the stains hinting at imagery, something with meaning trying to grow through.

I glanced at the bottle next to the bed and cursed the long-barreled .38 on the table beside the old rotary phone. The gun was scuffed and matte black; shiny nickel-plated revolvers need not apply.

An angry child had written on hotel stationary weighted down by the gun: Do It.

I lit a cigarette first, coughing as the smoke abused my lungs and feeling the rising tide of acid in my stomach. The bottle was some bottom-shelf whiskey I remembered buying at whatever Holiday I was drinking in last night.

Do It.

The black dog was really biting when I left myself notes like this. I'd read about it. It wanted me dead. Required medication. My solution was to drink until it left with its tail between its legs and I remained unkilled.

Do It.

I picked up the revolver, familiar with the weight, the electrical tape around the grip. I looked away when I thumbed back the hammer so I couldn't see if there was a round winking at me, rotating around the cylinder.

Sucking in a clawing drag from some ungodly Russian cigarette—*Jesus*—I parted the hair on my temple with the barrel.

Pulled the trigger.

The oily click meant that even while I was down in the hole I kept it in working order. That was a ritual too.

I stubbed out the cigarette in a Chinese take-out box and popped the cylinder to see a single round grinning up at me. The guy I was when I left the note had been serious.

In the shower I threw up between my feet and watched streaks of brown circle the drain.

- 3 -

I shaved and tightened up my appearance in the foggy mirror, pausing periodically to clean an arc of glass with the meat of my fist. I was neither good-looking nor ugly. A bit hungry looking. Maybe haunted.

I braced my hands on the cracked sink and ran water over a pair of scissors, watching tufts of blond hair clog the drain. The short haircut felt better.

My torso was lean and sinewy, but my forearms were the knotted appendages of a man who swung a hammer for a living. That was why I wore the long sleeve shirts and the jacket. The forearms didn't say average. The thick wrists said maybe a guy who spent too many hours hitting a heavy bag. Long sleeves covered that up. That and the rooster.

I grabbed a box of Clairol do-yourself-brunette and read the directions. Did myself.

- 4 -

I usually wore a suit because it was easy to blend in that way. This one was charcoal gray and the tie was black. The shirt was white. Maybe I was a copier repair type who needed to fancy up for the job but didn't quite have the knack.

If you know what to look for, the bend in my nose came from a fist. The scars over my eyes weren't terribly prominent but I bleed easily when hit. The longer the machine runs, the poorer it is at repairs, right? I didn't mind. Some guys thought that meant I was hurt. Would kick it into high gear to deliver the *coup de grace* when all that was happening was I'd sprung a leak.

Whatever advantage life offered, I took it.

I grinned at my reflection and brushed my teeth. Dental care was important. Used to be I looked older than my years. The mirror suggested I was catching up.

Back in the bedroom I could smell kitchen grease from The Quiet Man, the Irish pub on the first floor. The place was named after the John Wayne movie and a yellowed poster of the man himself was framed amidst the liquor bottles. They had it playing on a constant loop on a couple TVs. I'd seen it at least three times by this point.

If you knew who to ask, The Quiet Man had a few off-the-books rooms like the one I stayed in, not much to look at but clean, and the owner liked cash. The Irish were good for that in old-school towns like New York, Boston and Chicago. So many Micks hopped their visas to hit the bartender circuit. They took care of each other.

I hadn't been working much lately and Quiet had become a bit of a hangout. They knew me as John Gallo, an ID I reserved for friends. I'd drink downstairs. Maybe eat. Make my way upstairs to sleep until it was time to do it again. I wasn't one of them, but they were nice people and made me welcome.

My suitcase came out from under the bed, and I rolled my thumb over the combination lock until it popped open on the sweaty mess of blankets. The inside was filled with old socks and underwear. Not much of a ruse, but I was in the business of seconds.

My hand disappeared into the laundry and emerged with the

object of my desire. I freed it from its Ziploc prison and placed the bag back in the suitcase, the suitcase back under the bed.

The 9mm Beretta went into a shoulder holster.

- 5 -

I remembered my grandfather putting kittens into a potato sack and carrying them out to the driveway where his old Army car waited. He tied the sack to the exhaust pipe and went around to the driver's side where he keyed the ignition and lit a cigar, in that order. When the cigar was done so were the kittens, and he shut the car back down.

"How come you killed them?" I asked.

"Easiest way to get rid of 'em," he said.

"Why not get rid of the adult cats?"

"Need cats for the mice. Don't need kittens."

I was gone the next day. No one came looking.

It wasn't until the salty age of seventeen that I killed someone. Portuguese guy named Medeiros repaired shoes and had a shop in the Crown Heights part of Brooklyn. I thought it through the way I'd learned at the youth home, stole some gloves so I wouldn't leave prints and broke through a window to wait overnight in his shop. When it was time, I stuffed my gun hand into a leather boot and shot him through the heel. It was louder than I wanted but not too bad. One moment he was re-soling a lady's shoe and the next he was gone. He never knew I was in the shop. I heard footsteps overhead where he had an apartment. A little girl said the word, "Papai."

I left the way I came in.

The Dominican gal I was trying to impress called me *Gallo*, Spanish for Rooster, so I had the bird tattooed on my arm. Red and blue, the ink made it easy for a bookie to find me and give me five hundred dollars. I took a bus to Queens to kill a guy in Astoria. I thought it through again and took him off the count as easily as I did the cobbler. Word got around and I got a working name.

More and more people needed me and it felt good to be needed. Felt so good I forgot how bad off I was after wasting the cobbler. The tears. The shaking. Breaking a cherry is painful but it passes. I never felt bad about the ones after that first.

I worked for the Italians and the Russians. Did some jobs for the Chinese and once for a group of Yakuza. Money for a head. I began to move around the country, working. Thought more. Learned more. My price went up.

Everyone came to see the Rooster.

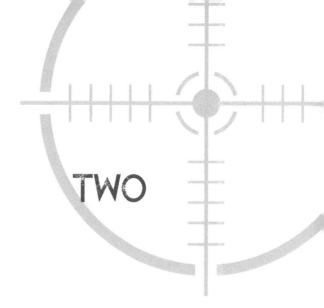

TWO

- 1 -

Anyone who wants my services has to know how to reach me. I only carry disposable cell phones and even those I trade out on a regular basis. They're too easy to track. And from what I read, all that blue light from the screen causes undue stress. I have enough of that as it is.

I was waiting in a filth-strewn apartment on a narrow street off of Bowery, kicking a path through the remains of someone's camp. Bottles, used condoms hardened into cement, sandwich wrappers crawling with ants. The area was up and coming, the old kitchen supply businesses and cheap flats making way for the life support system required by the workers of a new Silicon Alley, or so I had heard. An old man crept around in the apartment overhead, the only tenant left in the building. He was offered a cool million to move out so they could renovate, but the old bastard was hanging on for more if he could get it, bumbling around in an empty building as the hollow units below him filled with rats and dust.

I drew my finger along a dirty windowpane as I squatted in a cloud of smoke, perspiration stinging my eyes while I watched the street below. Patient. A spider crawled along the peeling sill, eight legs dark with city grime. Looking past the spider I saw a shining black Hummer pull up to the curb, brake lights glowing red, drawing attention.

Asshole.

I stood, knees popping, shaking out the pins and needles before I slipped out of the apartment as quietly as I'd entered.

The spider smoldered on the windowsill alongside the smoking butt, destroyed by the meteor of my descending cigarette.

- 2 -

He was the macho type and a virgin. He tapped the glass behind his head and the Hummer pulled out into traffic.

"You know who I represent," the guy said. Mr. Mystery. Would I be in the car if I didn't? I pulled out a cigarette, and a frown marred his chiseled features.

"I'd prefer you didn't—"

He pursed his lips as I stuck the cigarette in between my lips and lit it with a match. Asshole took the message I was delivering. Fuck you. And missed what I was concealing. A small tremor in my hands.

I dropped the match on the floor and we enjoyed the scent of singed carpet.

He was an attorney, some blend of European and Chinese in a fitted suit with gym-fed muscles. He was the type who had his haircut neatened every three weeks, probably lived on skinless chicken breasts and brown rice. When I saw the shoulder-holstered gun inside his jacket, I knew it was a message for me.

He just didn't know what he was saying.

I held his eyes through a rising ribbon of smoke while he tried to figure out whether blinking would make him look weak.

"I'm not gonna stick around for another butt," I told him, sucking in a lungful, drawing his eyes to the glowing orange tip.

He pulled the briefcase off the floor and onto his knees, waiting long enough to let me know he was making a decision when we both knew his employer had already made the decision.

"I have an envelope for you."

He popped the catches and opened the briefcase, pulling out a plain, white envelope. Inside was a handwritten note with stage directions. I understood why I wasn't dealing with the usual people.

"Can I drop you somewhere?"

Friends now. I said, "St. Regis."

He keyed an intercom button for the driver and said "Fifty-Fifth Street," before giving me an insider's smile. "Good choice."

"They know me."

We passed Fifty-Third Street and I flicked my head to the side. Chicken Breast tapped the glass again. The driver was a pro and eased us between two taxis before gliding to a stop at the curb.

I pushed open the door and stepped out as the lawyer said, "What should I tell—"

I closed the door and headed against the traffic before circling the block south until I caught an M4 bus heading north, standing room only. I banged my shin against a hard plastic seat and cursed, got off at the next stop and escaped the sun in the shadow of a newsstand. Reaching into a narrow glass case on the left of the kiosk to pull out a Coke gave me time to scan the street with my peripheral vision, and I touched two cans before I found one that was cold enough. The old guy behind the counter held up one finger without raising his eyes from the newspaper he was reading. I laid a dollar next to his elbow.

"You hear about the guy in Astor Place? Has a newsstand like yours?" I said, killing time.

He looked up at my question and the light caught his knit cap, done in alternating bands of green, black and yellow.

"They're closing him down after thirty years in the same spot," I continued.

"Rich people moving in, don't want the eyesore in their neighborhood," he said, his voice surprisingly soft and rich with West Indian currents.

"Eyesore?" I scanned the rack of magazines, *Sports Illustrated* next to *King*, *XXL* and *Maxim*. The latter three boasted covers themed around asses. I saw the *New York Times* and the *Post*. Okay, the *Post* was awful but what was the eyesore?

"Gentrification," he said and I nodded, saying, "Gentrification."

I popped the top on my Coke and walked away, thinking about the guys that work the coffee carts and newsstands. How some days they're the only people I exchange a word with.

There was a gap in traffic and I quick-stepped across the street, trying not to shake up my soda. A gypsy cab honked at me but I ignored it and hopped over a puddle to make the far sidewalk. Pigeons scattered from a busted muffin on the cement but returned to their feast once I passed.

I took another long sip and tossed the half-full can into a green trashcan before I reached a subway hole.

A downtown Six train was just arriving and the car I boarded was air conditioned. I even managed to get a seat.

THREE

There was a swampy texture to the night and I could feel sweat trickling down my ribs beneath my shirt. I passed the stink of the open-air fish markets on Canal and below the looming arch of the Manhattan Bridge spanning the East River, collapsing into the shoulder-to-shoulder press of Catherine Street until I reached East Broadway.

It started to rain.

I tried to imagine Chicken Breast down here as I pushed through the milling crowds on the neon-washed streets of Chinatown, periodically wiping away the water funneling into my eyes as Cantonese chatter filled the air. He was at least half Chinese or he wouldn't have had the gig but I doubt he felt much tie to this community. He was Soho and Tribeca all the way.

"Five dollah," an old lady said, fanning out DVDs in plastic sleeves. I shook my head and slipped around her, stepping into the gap behind a tourist couple.

Even in the rain there was a line to get into Jade Unicorn.

Hungry aspirants filled the lobby, staring up at the ring of the second-floor dining area as the aroma of Chinese dim sum drifted down to taunt and tantalize. The air was filled with the clatter of cutlery and voices competing in Cantonese and English.

Crowds have a Brownian movement and I pressed forward, shifting left or right as openings suggested themselves, earning a few irritated glances but nothing of note.

Tommy Xiao caught my eye and nodded toward the stairs and I met him there, shaking hands.

I don't do elevators if I can help it.

Up past the open ring of the second story to the third story, a vast, circular room of round tables where waitresses pushed carts filled with steaming delicacies. Up again, the stairs switching back as we neared the fourth-floor dining area, also nearly full. Waiters ran up and down the stairs carrying covered trays, leaving invisible, near narcotic scent trails in their wake. The stairs were impeccably clean, unlike the streets outside. The kitchen—I had been through it more than once—was equally sanctified.

I was led into the circus of the dining room, the tables draped in white, the ceilings high and decorated with glass chandeliers overhead. Someone in a white jacket offered a hand towel and I used it to dab my face dry, finger combing my wet hair. My raincoat was hung on a coat tree.

The gentleman waiting for me didn't stand as I was seated, a waiter tucking in my chair behind me. He was older but still keen-eyed, a fringe of iron grey hair shaved to stubble. I knew him as Mr. Chin.

He poured me a cup of aromatic tea and I sipped carefully while it cooled, neither of us speaking until two waiters rolled up a silver platter on which resided the succulent brown carcass of a duck. Mr. Chin exchanged rapid-fire Cantonese with the senior waiter and turned to me.

"*Gōng Jī*, would you like a Tsing Tao? Or an American beer?"

Gōng Jī meant Rooster and implied a gentle respect. He could have referred to me as *Jiào Jī*, which also meant rooster but was more commonly the slang term for visiting a prostitute.

"Whiskey. Suntory."

Did his eyes narrow before he nodded? The waiters set to work with gleaming knives, preparing small plates of duck meat and crispy skin. The duck would have been bred with this dish in mind and cooked in a special oven. The waiters assembled the meal on top of a small, pale pancake, wrapping it around slivers of scallion, cucumber and a dollop of sweet bean sauce along with choice pieces of the meat.

Mr. Chin detailed the job as I ate, speaking in English both for my benefit and to exclude the waiters. The job was simple enough, I had done such for Mr. Chin in the past. He asked me if I would like more duck and I declined, recognizing the dismissal.

The meal wasn't dinner. It was theater. My whiskey arrived and I knocked it back, relishing the smoky heat.

"Tommy will take care of your arrangements," he said and I stood, nodding before walking through the cavernous room and ignoring the restaurant staff present while collecting my raincoat. They understood that Mr. Chin's business required discretion.

I made my way down several flights of stairs past hurrying waiters. I was sweating from the alcohol.

When I reached the kitchen level, I walked past the clatter of pots and hissing woks and moved down a steamy, cement hallway reeking of ginger and garlic.

A windowless wooden door with a Chinese character stenciled on the outside was hidden at the end of the hall beside stacked cardboard boxes bulging with cabbages. I raised my hand to knock but heard commotion inside and pushed the door open, pausing at the flurry of movement, indistinct in the blue light of a computer screen.

"Shit, *Gōng Jī*," Tommy Xiao said, setting himself in the desk chair and flicking on a goose-necked accounting lamp. The girl walked around the desk with her eyes on the floor before taking a seat in one of the visitor's chairs.

"I thought you'd still be up there with the old man," he said, sliding a CD jewel case smeared with white powder off the desk and into a waiting drawer. I glanced at the girl, unable to see much of her in the low light. "Don't worry about her, she doesn't speak English."

He said something to her in French and she murmured, "*Oui*" as he spun in the chair and bent low to work the combination of a restaurant safe on the floor.

I drew the silenced Beretta and shot him in the spine. Even with the sound suppressor the gun made a metallic *clap* in the confined space. The girl shrieked as Tommy lurched from the chair onto his knees, hands pawing for the hole in his back. I sighted down the length of the barrel and put a round behind his ear. The bullet sounded like knuckles hitting a side of beef. A fan of red drops sprayed across a framed street map of Chinatown on the back wall.

The girl was pressed against the wall, her eyes round white smears in the dark. I angled the desk lamp to play over her. Watched her chest move as she took hurried sips of air and wondered about the ripped shoulder of her blouse. The drop of blood at the corner of her lips.

The Beretta lined up on her left eye.

"Who are you?" I asked. She had the kind of caramel skin casting directors like. A choose-your-ethnicity kind of gal.

She shook and I imagined the gun barrel was a mile wide in her view.

"I'm just an ac-ac-actress," she stammered out.

Her eyes rolled with terror and I holstered my pistol.

"Who else knows you're here? Tommy book you through a service?"

"No, no service. We just met."

I was only paid for one body. "They find out you were here, you're dead." I walked out.

FOUR

On the weekends even the Holiday Lounge would be mobbed with the bridge-and-tunnel crowd, but on a weeknight it was ugly enough to remain a local joint. I gave it another year or two before rising rents put it out of business.

I sipped a whiskey at the bar. Concentrated on the fiery burn spreading down my throat and throughout my chest while a couple of guys argued near the cigarette machine.

"Lookin' for a breakfast date?"

She wore the miles hard and her teeth were yellow even in the dim light. By 4:00 a.m., when the bars shut their doors, she'd be prime cut, but that magical hour was still a ways off.

I let my eyes do their thing. Her smile faltered.

"Hey—"

My eyes are dark and I've been told they don't reflect light the way eyes should. She moved off with a muttered curse, and Sal the bartender looked in my direction, smelling trouble.

I nodded for a refill.

He poured.

I sipped.

It burned.

It was years ago when I actually saw someone. A professional. I got the idea from a movie but I was curious and picked a city where

I didn't do much business, St. Louis, and found a guy. Paid him two hundred dollars to ask questions like: "Am I a sociopath?" and "Do I have multiple personalities?"

I told him how I felt taller when I worked. How I saw and heard more. I could sense the meat-locker cold of space and boiling heat of the sun. How I felt like someone who would listen to music with cellos and a woodwind section. The doctor told me that multiple personalities were rare, not like in the movies, but that heightened sensory input and sense of self during periods of high stress was not uncommon. I pressed him to explain how I could feel outer space. How I wanted to hear clarinets, not even really knowing what a fucking clarinet looked like, let alone sounded like.

That was an interesting conversation. He suggested terms like post-traumatic stress disorder. Depression. I left with ten minutes still on the clock and put two hundred and fifty miles between us. Spent the night in Kansas City where I ate ribs.

I was willing the fist around my heart to unclench when a hand touched my shoulder. I opened my eyes and saw her reflection in the warped mirror behind the bar.

"You're fucking kidding me."

Sal looked over again.

"I'm sorry..." she began before slumping onto the stool next to me. I got a better look at her then, light blouse over a black pencil skirt and stockings I expected to have a seam up the back. Club clothes for the kind of creep joint Tommy Xiao frequented in the Meatpacking District.

But even without the rip at the shoulder and the mussed hair, there was something off about her, as if she'd dressed to match magazine spreads a decade or more out of date.

"I didn't know what to do," she said.

There were people around. Noticing.

I put a bill down on the bar before beckoning the girl after me. We were outside at a crosswalk when she said, "I'm Ava."

FIVE

- 1 -

The cops had put the boot on a white van across the street from The Quiet Man. The hamstrung van was lost in a sea of identical, rusty vehicles in Red Hook's warehouse district and picking that one out struck me as unfair.

We stopped in the lee of a taco truck with a few construction types hunched near the serving window, working their way through what smelled like *asada* and *al pastor*. Rain pattered against the truck's extended awning overhead.

"Room's paid for through tomorrow," I said.

"Aren't you gonna stay?"

"Getting my things," I said and made my way through the door into The Quiet Man where the sour stink of beer replaced the aroma from the food truck. Half a dozen guys were playing darts and demolishing pitchers but the pool table was open. Frank nodded at me from his post at the bar and gave Ava an appreciative once-over when I led her back to the pay phone and through a green door marked No Admittance.

I led her up a narrow staircase that tilted to the left until we reached the third story. The hardwood floor of the hall was buckled and creaked beneath our shoes until I stopped at my room and checked that the tape on the bottom of the door was intact.

"What's the tape for?" Ava asked.

I opened the door and felt for the wall switch. The overhead bulb popped and went dark. I was blinking away the afterimage when I crossed to the window and felt the broken tape at the bottom.

"Out!" I shoved her at the door.

A warm wind lifted us into the hall.

- 2 -

A few groggy inhabitants staggered down the smoke-filled hallway and I pushed up to my feet, ears ringing. I touched my jaw where a mule had kicked it and blinked to stop the spinning. I had my gun in my hand.

Ava was on the floor, pale with plaster dust, moving on her back like butter just starting to slide on a skillet.

Who was she to me?

The door across the hall cracked open and a blue-jowled guy in black-rimmed glasses sat down hard, blood spurting from a hole in his sweatshirt. I hadn't heard the report of my gun but I felt it buck in my hand and caught the movement when a shotgun fell from his grip.

He was saying something and I shook my head before I fed him another piece of lead and he cut the chatter.

Ava was sitting with her head lowered like a groggy drunk. I grabbed a fistful of her blouse and dragged her into the room and over the still-warm corpse. She sprang to her feet like a scalded cat and pulled away from me.

She said something angry but I looked away and missed it, glad for the deafness as I walked over and across the narrow bed and looked out his window.

Fire escape. I banged out the screen and yanked her toward the window. She hiked the skirt up to climb through, slipping on the wet metal fire escape but catching the railing. She scuttled quickly down to the next platform and didn't wait for me, kicking the rusty ladder until it dropped with a clang that made it through the cotton in my ears.

I ran back over to the dead man and took his shotgun before following Ava into the rain.

SIX

- 1-

The rolling sound was made by a Gatorade bottle filled with urine as it migrated back and forth across the floor of the subway car, the train rattling over the Williamsburg bridge toward the shimmering lights of Manhattan. I had no destination in mind beyond escaping Red Hook. Needed time to think.

Ava was staring out the window at the glow of the city, smeared by filthy windows. I adjusted the shotgun under my raincoat, trying for comfort and concealment, but they didn't want to give me a package deal. She mistook it for an invitation and clutched my sleeve. I plucked her hand off my arm.

I looked at her, really looked at her, wondering what her presence meant. The rain had left a ghostly outline of dust on her cheekbones and beads of water decorated her black hair. Her blouse was damp enough to show the outline of a dark bra beneath. She was holding a pair of strappy heels in her free hand and put them on the seat next to her.

"What's your name?" she asked, returning my look as the train rattled over the river far below. I thought about telling her the water would be cold and dark, even in summer at high noon. About the current that would suck you out into the cargo shipping lanes. A shark or two had been spotted in the Hudson River but never in the

East River. Nothing lived in it. Used to be where the mob dumped the bodies. It was dead water, fit only for corpses.

The black dog was still too close. Made me too introspective. I needed to hole up and get drunk, eat greasy food delivered to my room until I could function again.

Or until I left myself another note and got lucky with a trigger pull.

The overhead speaker buzzed with something that might have been, "Next stop, Essex."

If I had left her right there, things might have gone down differently.

- 2 -

I tossed the shotgun on the room's single bed.

"He didn't get you through a service?"

The toilet was running and the wallpaper was sticky to the touch, but we were on the top floor, the fifth, and what I could see of the street through the security mesh was sparsely peopled. An empty pigeon's nest adorned the sill outside, tufted with grey feathers. I hoped the birds wouldn't return home for the night.

"I'm not a prostitute." She hugged her arms around herself.

It was a small hotel up in Inwood near the top of Manhattan, a single train stop across the river from the Bronx. A mixed neighborhood, we were in the part that spoke Spanish. The owner was an old orthodox man with ringlets of grey *peyot* hanging down alongside his seamed face. He took my cash and I took a room.

"I met him at a club," she was saying, eyes tracing yellow stains on the peeling wallpaper as the radiator emitted a tuberculin gurgle. "He said he had a gram, invited me back to party."

"Coke whore is still a whore."

She circled the sunken bed and into the bathroom. Closed the door while I looked out the window and wondered if the rain would stop. A curling strip of fly paper heavy with the dead was hanging from the ceiling, close enough to touch my cheek. I moved away.

The toilet flushed and the sink ran before Ava emerged from the bathroom.

"I will shoot you in the face if you lie to me," I said. "You wearing a wire? Got a piece?"

Ava froze, staring down the barrel of my Beretta for the second time that night. I'd screwed the silencer onto the weapon while she had the door closed.

"I'm not wearing a wire. I won't lie to you." Her voice steady but her eyes not moving, pupils fixed points on the black hole at the end of the suppressor.

"I'm gonna pat you down."

She shook her head. "You still won't be sure." Her eyes went hard and held on to mine while she kicked off her heels and reached back to unzip the fitted skirt. She moved her hips from side to side and worked the skirt down until it pooled at her feet. She wore stockings gartered at the thigh. Black bikini briefs.

I twitched the barrel of the pistol and she unbuttoned her blouse until it slid off her shoulders and hit the floor. The bra was black and hooked in front. Her face didn't move as she undid the catch and the bra opened, her breasts swinging free. She bent at the waist and pushed the stocking down her thigh to her ankle and worked it off with her other foot. She repeated the process and then slid the briefs down over her hips, stepping out of them when they reached her feet.

I saw something in her eyes, saw that my hunger was visible, so I lowered the pistol until it was aimed at her heart.

"Lift 'em," I said and she cupped her breasts, lifting until I could see the black lines in a half crescent beneath their curve. Her nipples were dark and outlined by tattooed stars with too many points.

"What is that?"

"Calligraphy beneath my breasts. Mandalas around my nipples."

"Some kind of voodoo tattoo shit?"

"Some kind."

"I can't read it."

"It's a curse," she said and the whites of her eyes went grey.

"Turn around," I said and she did.

"Over to the bed," I said, and I could smell the scent of her as she walked past. Clean sweat. A little booze. Her hips rolled, but I didn't think she was putting anything into the effort.

She sat on the bed gingerly, as if it would evaporate as suddenly as the rest of her reality had. It squeaked when she moved.

I leaned the shotgun in a corner.

"You smart?" I asked.

"Yes."

"Get dressed," I said after patting down the pile clothes and dropping them on the bed.

She did, unfazed by my presence, but jumped when I locked a handcuff around her wrist, snapping the other end to the bed's headrail. Her lips tightened and she leaned away like the game had gone somewhere she didn't trust.

"You don't need this," she said.

"You were right before. I'm still not sure, but I need to sleep."

My hand found the wall switch and turned off the room's only light. I slid down against the wall beside the shotgun and let my eyes close.

I could hear my breathing and pictured a door lined with a hundred padlocks. Schlages and Yales scattered between manual deadbolts. I saw my hands starting at the top of the door and closing the hasp of a padlock. Felt the heavy metal in my palm. The click of the mechanism locking home. I let my fingers trace the wood, felt the splinters in the frame before they reached the first deadbolt and slid it closed.

"Why were you there tonight?" Her question was quiet, but my image of the door began to distort. A sandcastle in a strong wind.

"Go to sleep," I said.

I imagined another lock. Silver. Yale stamped on the side.

"I'm cold," she whispered.

SEVEN

Orange light drifted like mist between the dingy brick buildings and through the grimy window of the hotel.

Ava sat up under a tangled sheet when the plastic bag landed beside her. I'd already been out and back.

"Put this stuff on," I said. "You can't walk around in club clothes."

I bent to release her cuff, noticing that the rusty headrail was unmarred where the cuff circled it. She hadn't even tried to break free.

She rubbed circulation back into her wrist and shoulder.

"What?" she asked. Some of last night's fear evaporated but challenge hadn't returned to her eyes.

I sat on the corner of the room's lone table.

"I don't even know your name," she said.

I set to work on the shotgun, using my new saw to shorten the barrel and the butt. A scatter gun would play merry hell in narrow hallways and cramped apartments.

Ava sat on the bed nearer to me, something odd in her attitude. "I don't care that you killed Tommy. He turned out to be a real sleaze."

I worked quickly, wrapping clothesline around the sawed-off stock to rig a sling. I had three rounds for the scatter gun. One partial magazine for the Beretta and another with fifteen rounds in a sleeve of the shoulder holster. Still had a straight razor in my sock.

"So?" she said.

I switched out the partial clip for the full one, the brass winking up at me.

"Take a shower now or you won't get one. I've got one stop to make then I'm putting you on a train back to Pigsnout or wherever the hell you came from."

Ava stood up.

"I'm not going back."

"Not an option," I said, my flat stare draining the weird light from her eyes.

Her shoulders drooped and she turned, walking to the bathroom with the plastic bag. She looked back.

"I still don't know what your name is."

"Rooster."

I listened to the shower running, thinking about Ava's changing attitudes and wondering why I hadn't already killed her.

The bathroom door was thin and weak. Even locked it wouldn't stop me.

I plucked the silencer from my pocket and threaded it onto the barrel. Blood would wash down the drain. Clean up would be minimal.

The rushing sound of the shower ceased.

Ava emerged from the bathroom wearing the new clothes and smelling like soap. Her eyes locked on the pistol and I saw goosebumps spring up on the bare skin of her arms.

I gestured to the bed.

She sat wearily and I cuffed her wrist to the headrail. Gave the bed frame a tug. Flimsy.

"Why do you keep locking me up?"

"I don't know."

EIGHT

- 1 -

I caught a downtown A train and breathed through my nose when the lights dimmed and we stopped in between stations, reminding myself not to step on the third rail if we were hit here and I had to play tunnel rat. This wasn't paranoia, just readiness, I reminded myself.

Something fuzzy and unintelligible dribbled from the speakers overhead and we were moving a minute later. The door between cars cycled open and a man in baggy pants and a sweatshirt hit my car. "I am an Iraq veteran," the panhandler called out, clinging to a pole. "I'm sorry to bother you but…"

I tuned him out with everyone else.

The cop got on at 181st Street and leaned against the doors, sullen and thick-faced, equipment belt creaking. I fished a dollar out of my pocket and used the movement to clock the cop, but he was studiously avoiding eye contact with the panhandler, having discovered something intriguing beneath his thumbnail.

The cop got off at 163rd Street, but I stayed onboard until Forty-Second Street, using the chaos of the Times Square Station to peel off anyone tracking me before catching another train back uptown. I slumped back in my seat, knees wide, someone who had been on the train too long and would be on it for much longer. The eternal passenger, part of the scenery.

At 125th Street I stood abruptly and got off with the crowd, using the exposed elevated platform to look around Harlem and reconsider my options, but coming up with the same answer. Still had no idea who came after me at The Quiet Man but didn't think it was Chin, an old-school racist who preferred to work with his own people unless it was time to call in a trained dog to perform a specific task. A special task like taking out his own lieutenant, Tommy Xiao.

I'd been so quiet lately that a hit on me didn't make any sense.

I leaned on the railing and enjoyed a breeze, looking into bedroom windows five or six stories up. Didn't see much of interest. Guy was laying on his back, shades open, his gut like a burial mound. Bet the fucker was hot. Didn't care who saw, just needed to breathe.

Pigeons fluttered up from the roof nearest me and I turned my gaze inward. The attack in Red Hook was violent but sloppy.

"Fuck."

Too many variables, but I had to write off the gear and funds left behind at The Quiet Man, blown to so many cinders. I needed the payment from the Xiao hit and that meant keeping an appointment in the park.

I pulled out my burner phone and opened up the web browser, selecting an unlocked Wi-Fi network named Federal Body Inspector when it offered itself up. I don't trust email but it's impossible to exist without it in my line of work. If I need to book a quick flight, rent a car off-site, I needed email. This was one of my real addresses, the one Grace used if she wanted me to get in touch.

There was nothing from Grace, but Christian singles wanted to meet me and a pill would cure my erectile dysfunction. There was a Travelocity notice sent to the name attached to the email address but it was a deal I could afford to miss.

THE QUIET MAN.

My heart stuttered when I read the subject line. The sender's address was meaningless gibberish, but…

I clicked open the email and saw an attached video file. If this was some kind of phishing attempt they wouldn't get much, so I opened the file.

It was dark, the footage recorded by some kind of night-vision camera so I didn't recognize the room at first. I'd never seen my room above the bar from the angle of the camera, anyway.

The door opened and I saw myself enter, eyes glowing weirdly in the green footage. I saw myself crossing the room, checking the tape I'd left at the window. Turning. Running. The image rocked and everything disappeared in a flare of light.

A breath I didn't know I was holding exploded from me and I slumped against the railing, taking the weight on my elbows.

I thumbed the volume up to maximum and replayed the video. "Our boy from Brighton Beach tried to snuff the Rooster," a woman crooned over the video of me entering the room. The voice was electronically distorted but the cheer in her words left me cold. On screen the room went white and I recalled the numbing blast. "The Rooster is running and it's up to you. Who's it gonna be, boys? Who's it gonna be?"

A train rattled past the platform behind me and the crash of metal jolted me from my reverie.

I grabbed the phone in both hands and twisted abruptly, snapping the cheap plastic frame. I had no idea if the video was sent to taunt me or to hold me in place while some kind of Trojan horse activated a GPS to broadcast my location.

Our boy from Brighton Beach. Had to be Russians, the Little Odessa mob. Why were they after me?

I tossed the broken phone in a trashcan and quick-stepped to the long staircase, pushing past a couple ascending side by side and drawing an angry look. My boots clattered as I hustled down as quickly as I could without drawing attention.

Without looking like I was running.

- 2 -

I headed west toward the Hudson, hitting a corner bodega that didn't carry Viceroys so I bought a pack of Parliaments from a turbaned Sikh who called me, "My brother."

I stopped to peel off the plastic wrapper and glanced around for anyone paying too much attention to me. For someone filming with a cell phone. I thought about orbiting satellites with cameras so powerful they could read the license plate on a car.

There are no damned satellites tracking me. Knock it off.

I dropped the wrapper into a trashcan on the corner while a spotted dog marked it as his own, the woman holding the leash looking east while I looked west.

We moved on in those directions.

There was a garbage strike in the city and the black trash bags were piled higher than my head along the edge of the sidewalk, a rancid ridgeline baking in the sun. They reduced some sidewalks to narrow canyons with people living on one side and their refuse on the other. When I broke free I sucked in fresh air blowing in off the river and read a sign informing me that there was no smoking in the park. A yellow cab honked behind me. I ducked my head against the wind and lit a new cigarette.

Our boy from Brighton Beach tried to snuff the Rooster.

The attack was sloppy but the camera meant planning. It didn't add up.

There are no satellites.

But there was planning.

Who's it gonna be boys? Who's it gonna be?

Elm trees in Riverside Park threw shadows across the grass outcrops as the sun reached east across the choppy expanse of the Hudson River to light defiant the New Jersey shoreline in shades of yellow and orange. The breeze stirred up the mulchy odor of fallen leaves, and I passed a few joggers lost in the world of their headphones. A dog walker was struggling with four mutts pulling in different directions, and a cluster of businessmen had architectural tubes on a picnic table as one spread out some kind of drawing.

I headed up along the river walk, giving any tails plenty of time to show themselves, working my way through the pack and wishing they were Viceroys. I left a trail of matches in lieu of breadcrumbs.

I went off the path and over a rocky bulge to see a small, cement building housing public restrooms in the lee of the old stone retaining wall. Ghost letters of forgotten signage appeared amidst the scrawled graffiti, but even so, the functional old wall conveyed an elegance of construction that made the more modern restroom building that squatted in its shadow even uglier in comparison.

She was like that, New York. The past peeking through to the present almost like an invitation to walk through a veil and step into a more refined day. It calmed me to study her.

I blew my nose into a Kleenex, glanced at the result out of habit and stuck the wad of tissue in my coat pocket.

Normally any job I did for Chin was paid out by Tommy, but the old man had made other arrangements to keep the target out of the loop. Tommy had been skimming. Tommy had been sharing secrets. Chin wanted him dead and tapped me for the gig.

Was Chin trying to clean up after I did Tommy?

The old man's arrangements were needlessly complex, but that was how Chin's mind operated, giving weight to the rumors that he had once worked for the intelligence services in the People's Republic. The attack in Red Hook would have embarrassed him with its inelegance. He believed in dead drops and tradecraft. Cyanide teeth.

I sat on a rock and lit another cigarette, watching the building.

Who's it gonna be boys?

It was a beautiful morning for pondering so I thought about the voice attached to the video and tried to picture the woman, but all I could imagine was a robot, chrome-skinned and neon-eyed.

When no one had walked by in five minutes I tossed the butt onto the grass and entered the men's room.

Inside was an alchemical stink of piss and disinfectant, grime and graffiti covering every surface. Two of the yellow ceiling lights were out and the remaining unit buzzed intermittently, as if it too wanted to leave. It was a room that benefited from low lighting so I didn't mind, but a working fan would have been nice.

I held my breath and entered a stall, closing the door before crouching to peel aside a wall tile with a scrawled bit of graffiti, presumably Chinese. The dead drop held a plastic Ziploc sandwich bag and a roll of bills.

I pocketed the money and froze at the sound of the outer door to the building opening.

Footsteps.

The sound of a zipper.

Pissing.

I stepped out of the stall and saw a Japanese businessman in an overcoat busy at one of the urinals. A poster tube was leaning against the wall near his knee. One of the architects I'd seen earlier.

The man didn't glance up as I walked past him and out the door—

The kick was lighting fast, from someone standing right around the corner. I doubled over and the shotgun spilled free as I stumbled back into the men's room.

Two more Japanese businessmen pushed inside and grabbed my arms, while Overcoat crossed from his position at the urinal and ripped the Beretta from my shoulder holster. I bucked back and tried to kick him in the crotch, but he was fast and swept my foot aside with his shin.

He pivoted his hip and powered a straight kick into my gut. I flew back into a urinal hard enough to rip it from the wall.

Black spots danced across my vision as I crumpled, trying to suck in a breath. I lifted my head to see Overcoat open the plastic poster tube and draw forth a short, curved sword, the glittering blade maybe a foot and a half in length.

He barked in Japanese and his two compatriots pulled me to my knees. Something in my brow split when they shoved my head into the floor and a hot spill of blood spattered the filthy tiles.

Overcoat lifted the sword with ritual slowness, muttering in guttural fury, not noticing my left hand crawling back toward my ankle.

The sword reached its azimuth, edge razor sharp—

I slashed one man behind the knee and twisted hard, dragging the straight razor through the Achilles tendon of the other.

They howled and collapsed. One tripped over my back to impede the swordsman's stroke. We rolled together for a bit and I slithered onto the man's belly, grinding his suit against the filthy floor before swiping the blade across his carotid artery.

He cried out and tried to hold back the tide of blood as I surged to my feet and slashed wildly, backing the swordsman up.

I spat a red wad of mucus onto the floor. The swordsman flinched and reset himself.

"Who the fuck are you?" I asked.

The swordsman shook his head and I dropped to one knee, burying the straight razor to the hilt in the other man's neck while rolling over his body.

A red fountain, so beautiful.

The men's room smelled like a butcher shop with an open sewer running through the middle. Whatever we were in life, we were ugly in death.

The swordsman was rattled, I could see it as he settled deeper into his stance, bracing himself. This wasn't like training in a dojo. Clean floors. Starched clothes. This was grime and shit and a humiliating death in a public toilet.

Home sweet home.

I backed away and he stepped forward, hesitating at the still-twitching body of the guy trying to swallow my razor. He stepped over the dying man and I spun toward the sinks, snatching up the slippery rim of a metal wastebasket and torquing at the hips to throw it at the swordsman. He ducked and slipped in the blood as the trashcan clipped his shoulder. The sword fell to the floor and he stumbled, jacket stained with refuse.

I rushed him, but the sonofabitch spun into a judo throw and hurled me across the room. I demolished a stall.

He lunged for his fallen sword, but I threw myself on the smaller man, smashing his head into the hard wall. He slumped and I grabbed a fistful of hair, banging his skull off the cinderblock until it was as soft as an infant's fontanelle, his death poem written on the tiles in crimson.

I sank to my knees in pain. Gasping for air. Crawled to the swordsman's corpse and tore open his shirt to reveal a mess of colorful tattoos.

Yakuza.

I found my Beretta and levered myself up on the sink.

I ran.

NINE

Ava jerked awake when the hotel room door crashed open.

"What happened?"

"Why the fuck are you still here?" I snarled.

She recoiled, jerking against the cuff. I noticed something scrawled on the wallpaper over the bed. Dried brown the color of blood and difficult to read. Too exhausted to worry about it I tossed her the key and staggered to the bathroom to study my battered appearance in the mirror.

"Fuck."

The bathroom smelled worse, whatever was between the walls growing a fuzzy new layer. Becoming something new.

Ava filled the doorway.

"Is it the same guys?"

I let the raincoat slide off my shoulders and puddle at my feet. Peeling off my shirt drew a hiss of pain.

"Sonofabitch," I said, exhaling through my teeth as I probed the ugly bruises forming on my torso. I saw white flashes behind my eyes when I pushed against a rib.

"Will you talk to me?" Ava demanded.

I looked at her and she recoiled from whatever expression I wore.

I breathed and gained a sliver of control.

"There's money in the pocket of my coat," I said. "Take some and get out."

"But…you're hurt…I can…"

"You can what?"

I loomed toward her and she shrank back into the bedroom.

"I have a problem here and I don't need baggage. So what the fuck can you do?"

"I want to help. I just want to help…"

She covered her face with her hands and sank to the edge of the bed.

"I don't have anywhere to… I can't go back… You don't know… Shit!" she said, her accent growing thicker. Something exotic buttering the words.

I stared at her, waiting.

"You're just like all of them. Bastards who use you and throw you away." She stood up and her voice crackled with anger. "But you just skipped right ahead to throwin' me away! What's wrong with me?"

She tried to press herself against me and kiss my chest but I shoved her back, hard.

Ava bounced across the bed and struggled up to her feet. Someone in the room next door banged on the wall, and I fought down the urge to plow a few rounds through the plaster.

"Are you gonna hit me now?"

I stared.

"I know how to take a punch, don't you worry," she said, that weird light in her eyes again, along with the anger. "What do you want? Gut punch?"

Ava let the towel fall to the floor.

"Come on, big man! Is this what it takes to finally get your motor runnin'?"

She stepped forward, scrunching her eyes closed.

"C'mon! Do it!"

I backed up a pace, eyes never leaving her face. She stood on point, quivering with tension, eyes shut.

"Do it," she said, and the words sent a chill coursing through me as I remembered the note I'd left for myself.

"Leave," I said.

"I can't."

"Why?"

"I'm in trouble. I can't go back."

I shook my head and walked into the bathroom. Touched my face. Fingertips coming away bloody.

Ava tossed a small glassine bag on the sink. "It helps if you're hurt." She was holding the towel in front of her.

I stared and she returned my gaze silently, sensing that any sound would send things the wrong way. "Where'd you get the coke?"

"Stole it from Tommy."

I picked up my coat and fished out cash from the pocket.

"Go to the corner and get some medical tape, rubber bands, alcohol and chewable Tylenol. And get me a duffle bag and T-shirt or something."

"Are you gonna be here when I get back?"

"Just get the stuff."

She nodded, but I grabbed her arm.

"You have to do exactly what I say, every minute, every second. Got it?"

"I will."

I eased myself down onto the bed and faced the thought I'd been avoiding. New York had gone bad. I didn't know who and didn't understand why, but there was a price on my head. It was time to run. Leave town. It wasn't paranoia, it was real.

"Who's it gonna be boys," I whispered and lay back beneath another phrase written in blood and imagined it a curse as my mind wandered back along the years. The orthodox guy who owned the building reminded me of another man from the neighborhood who'd been a victim. Not that I gave him a second thought. My business had been with his killer.

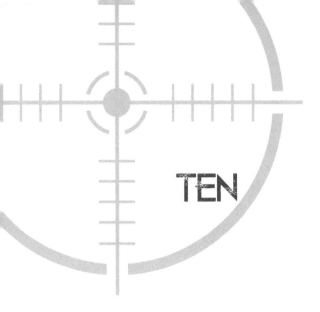

TEN

- 1 -

Some of this I saw and the rest of it I was told. It was four years ago. This is what went down.

Spanish pulled a thin leather glove over the knuckles of his right hand, the other glove held in his white teeth until he adjusted the first to his satisfaction. He repeated the process with his left as the bearded man tied to the chair squirmed, rattling the wooden legs on the peeling linoleum of the kitchen floor. He was trying to speak around the gag, the bearded man, but Spanish was busy.

They called him Spanish because he could pull a confession out of anyone. An Inquisition reference, right? Tall and narrow-hipped, he favored tight gray slacks with flared cuffs and a loose, cream-colored shirt. When he looked in the mirror he thought, "Toreador," and spun as he imagined a bullfighter might.

A poncho was waiting for him with a vaguely Mexican design; it furthered the image and kept his shirt clean.

It was all about communicating, everything. That's what the Oracle told him that first day in Queens, in a kitchen not unlike the one in which he stood today. He didn't know about the babysitter camera they had hidden on the shelf. Or he did know and geared his performance toward it. He was a showman.

"Three weeks late, Moishe," Spanish said to the bearded man.

"Three weeks late and you talkin' everywhere like you ain't gonna pay what you owe."

The old Hassid's eyes bulged with his effort to speak, his beard bristling as if with electricity.

Spanish stood on tiptoes and set the overhead lamp in its glass shade to swinging. It would be disorienting, he thought. Look like a movie.

"So you said your bit, now you ready to hear what the Oracle's got to say?"

Moishe nodded furiously, sweat pouring down his face.

Spanish sniffed and stepped in with a stiff jab that broke the old Hassid's nose. Blood splashed out and hit the poncho as Spanish twisted at the hips and knocked the bound man onto the floor with a crash, chair and all. He heard pounding on the ceiling from the apartment below as he righted Moishe with a grunt of effort.

"You ready to listen?" Spanish said.

Moishe nodded, bloody and weeping.

"You got something to say?" Spanish asked.

Moishe nodded furiously and Spanish slipped fingers beneath the gag, dragging it down over the old man's bottom lip.

"Please, please," Moishe said, and the words emerged through bubbles of blood.

Spanish grinned, "You look like the Sunday funnies, you know, they got the words coming out in bubbles?"

Moishe didn't understand him or didn't hear, just kept repeating, "I'll pay, I'll pay. I have the money—"

"Whoa whoa whoa," Spanish said, backing up and holding his hands out in a warding gesture. "Shhhhh." He leaned forward and jerked the gag back into Moishe's mouth.

"Oracle don't give two shits anymore, Moishe. That's the message, right? You're too fucking late."

Spanish turned to where the wife was tied up on another kitchen chair he'd liberated from their table. She was slumped and motionless with a pillowcase over her head, but the swinging lamp made her shadow jump from wall to wall. "Too fucking late."

Spanish sniffed and set to work.

- 2 -

He peeled off the bloody gloves and wrapped them in the soiled poncho as he hurried down from the third-floor walk-up. He pushed out the door of the old tenement and down the short flight of steps to the cracked sidewalk. The bodies would be found soon enough.

You pay what you owe.

He sauntered west on 213th Street and when he saw a gutter he liked, kicked the gory gloves down the drain. The poncho found a new home in a dumpster a block later. They were low buildings here, three stories, sometimes four. He tried to read a faded sign painted on a brick wall but was distracted by his own reflection in a glass storefront. He slowed his walk to check himself out.

Ten minutes later he was on a downtown C train to Thirty-Fourth Street where he'd left his Ford near Penn Station. A couple of black guys moved down the car in between the passengers and did a fair doo-wop act, earning some quarters. They gave Spanish one look, the way he held onto the pole overhead and let his body sway with the train, and passed him by without holding out the hat.

At Thirty-Fourth Street he hopped off the train and joined the human millipede trudging up the stairs through a miasma of urine and marijuana smoke. He waved a hand in front of his face as the crowd dispersed along the broad sidewalk. New York could be disgusting when it wanted to be.

The phone booth was covered in loops of graffiti but wasn't otherwise too befouled and he dropped a dime, dialing a number in Queens that rang a dozen times before he hung up. A bum asked him for change and he sniffed, staring at the bent man until he shuffled away.

"Disgusting," he said to himself.

His car was a beautiful yellow machine with elegant fins, shining bright against the drab city grime in a way that just screamed *class*. He smirked at the ticket under his wiper blade and dropped it in the street before climbing behind the wheel. Adjusted the rearview mirror and reached up to smooth his hair.

"Shit."

All that business in a stuffy tenement and he'd worked up a sweat. A half circle of perspiration darkened the fabric beneath his armpit. A quick glance at the other arm confirmed that the infraction had occurred on both sides.

He keyed the ignition and spun the FM dial until he found Tito Puente, rolled down the window and looked over his left shoulder until a delivery truck gave him an opening and he eased into the flow. He'd have to stop in Brooklyn for a change of clothes.

He was so busy looking at himself that he never saw me, dogging him all the way from 213th Street.

- 3 -

Drops of water struck the phone as Spanish tapped in a number. He was naked after his shower and enjoying the breeze that billowed the curtains of his fifth-story apartment.

After a shower he preferred to air dry. Better for his skin. If people across the street got a show, that was all right.

He was God's gift, you know?

Spanish hung up, puzzled but not too much. Thought she must have had a run of clients. Wives who wanted to know whether their husbands were cheating. Young men who wanted to know if a girl would say, "yes." Madame Christina, the Oracle of Astoria, also known as Greektown.

She found him when he was still Kowalski, showed him how to recreate himself. How everything about him could and should deliver a message. She gave him the name Spanish and spread the word about his abilities. Brought him deeper and deeper into her loan-sharking business until he was the only one she needed.

She was all *he* needed, somewhere between mother and lover, teacher and friend. She lavished him with knowledge and gifts and he killed for her.

After several years passed by, she revealed that she was not Greek but a Cypriot, from an island perpetually torn between Greece and Turkey. He found out with a little digging of his own that she was actually a Turk through and through. That did nothing for her business so she became Greek.

Her fortune telling was a front but also seasoning for the character she portrayed. It didn't take much to spread the word through the Greek criminal set that she knew more than she should about people. Saw when someone was going to move against her before they even considered it themselves.

Her reputation spread.

Spanish opened up both closet doors and considered pants. Chose black, tight at the hips, flaring at the bottom over sharp-toed boots.

He spun through a few dance steps and debated a red shirt, which would be great for the clubs later that night but a bit much for business. He settled on blue linen so he could avoid any more sweat stains. Slipped a five shot .32 revolver into the belt at the small of his back and put on a black leather vest over that. A stiletto went into his right boot.

The radio was chattering about the war in Afghanistan and he shut it off. Spanish didn't give two shits about Afghanistan save one thing: he didn't have to go. She saw to that.

He shuffled and shifted his hips in place as music drifted in from the street while he tried calling Christina again. Got nowhere and decided to just head on over. If she was with a client, he'd use the back stairs and wait in her apartment.

- 4 -

He left his car on the street. A bell began its mournful tolling as he passed the broad front steps of a Greek Orthodox Church, and he glanced up to see if there was a wedding but saw only closed doors bound in iron. The neighborhood was crawling with churches, Greeks for the most part, but a bunch of Pope lovers as well.

He stopped in at a counter where they knew him and tapped a manicured nail against the glass, that damned bell still tolling outside. They wrapped a couple of spanakopita in wax paper, dropped them into a paper sack. Waved him away and a young man he knew as

Kasper said things like, "Your money's no good here!" when he tried to pay.

They knew him.

It was a half-and-half street, storefront businesses and two or three stories of apartments above. Not a lot of cabs in the neighborhood, mostly families. He looked through the grimy glass of a *New York Times* box on the corner and took in the headlines. More Afghanistan. He walked on.

The sign was still lit in the plate glass window, Madame Christina's — Fortunes Told in garish purple neon. Spanish could never wear purple though; he was too pale.

He slipped around the corner through the alley, avoiding the wet channel that ran down the middle and cursing a rat that darted across his path.

The staircase in back shook as he took it two steps at a time until he stood on the small platform outside the door. He hated how many keys he had to carry because they ruined the line of his pocket, but Christina was a big believer in security. So, he fished out the ring and went down the locks. Only the bottom lock on the knob itself was secured and he opened the scratched metal door, stepping through into darkness.

He flipped the wall switch and nothing happened. "Shit." Felt his way through the pitch black and wished she wouldn't pull the curtains all the time. He found the kitchen table by touch and tossed the keys on it. Heard them land, slide and fall off the edge. "Dammit. He stepped carefully, scuffing his boots across the tiles as he made his way toward the sink and the light overhead.

He sniffed and his useless eyes grew wide at the thick stink of body odor.

"Who—"

A rush in the darkness more heard than seen and then hands were on him, grabbing and punching. He lashed out screaming, "Do you know who I am?" and reached for the gun at his back but felt it snatched away before his questing fingers could find it. A wild fist collided with his jaw and his knees went weak.

He went down beneath a dogpile.

"Turn on a light!" a hoarse voice shouted as a cloth sack was pulled over his head. He struggled when they hauled him up but was punched in the kidney for his efforts. He went limp as they half-carried him, boot heels dragging on the tiles. They sat him in a chair and tied him to it.

He heard male voices. Something squeaking as it was wheeled into the room. Smelled smoke.

"Do you know who I am," he snarled, and they snatched off the hood in answer.

His eyes were drawn to the round, black metal of a charcoal grill on a tripod of metal legs. The kind of thing a family might use for a backyard cookout on the Fourth of July. Billows of white smoke rose from it, and he could feel the warmth of smoldering coals. See the shimmer of heat in the air over its open mouth. A fire alarm started beeping, and he heard muffled curses until it stopped.

Spanish coughed and his eyes watered. He blinked away tears and tried to understand what he saw beyond the charcoal grill. "Christina!" Spanish shouted and she shook in place, bound to a chair as he was. They had stripped her naked save for a cloth gag in her mouth, and her black hair was wild around her face. Her mouth worked and she made unintelligible sounds.

"We know who you are," an old man's voice said, the words thickened by a life in the Aegean. Spanish saw a broad-shouldered, bearded man in elegant red robes with gold crosses. His eyes burned beneath thick, black brows, and the hair on his head was the color of iron. He was a priest. Greek Orthodox. Spanish knew him.

"We know who you are," another old man said, also bearded, a yarmulke on his balding head. He was clad in a black suit with a thigh-length coat, a white cloth draped around his neck, the Star of David stitched into it at both ends.

Behind the rabbi and the Orthodox priest, Spanish saw several young men with hard eyes. Among them the same young Kasper who had told him his money was no good.

"You're hurting our people," the Greek said.

"You're hurting our people," the rabbi said.

Beads of greasy sweat slid down his face, but Spanish pushed a strangled laugh between his teeth. "A priest and a rabbi walk into a bar," he said, flashing his bright, white teeth.

The crowd behind Christina milled and parted as another old man walked through. He wore a conservative black suit with a flash of white at the collar and carried several andirons from the fireplace in Christina's living room.

Spanish tried to continue the joke but could produce only a dry, clicking sound. The Catholic priest shoved the metal tips of three andirons into the coals, stirring them so the heat in the crowded room rose noticeably. Spanish felt his bladder let go.

"You're hurting our people," the priest said, his accent honeyed with Roman vowels. "And we have decided to send a message."

"I understand, I understand, really I do—"

A fist struck his ear and Spanish stopped babbling.

"Not for you, little fish," the Greek said, admiring the coals. "This will be a message heard by all of your kind."

"No-no-no—" A work-roughened hand covered his mouth until a dish towel was stuffed between his teeth, deep enough that he nearly choked.

The kitchen lights went off then and the three old men were lit from below in cruel, flickering orange. It was a vision from an older time, terrifyingly pagan. The firelight drew harsh lines on their faces as they looked at Spanish. Their eyes caught the glow of the coals, shining as if lit by Hell itself.

The three holy men each lifted an andiron, and Spanish could not keep his eyes from darting back and forth between them.

"We will send such a message," they said in unison.

Spanish screamed through the gag as the glowing orange tips of the hot irons floated toward him.

I waited outside until the screaming died to whimpering and pushed in through the door, ski mask over my face. My job was less dramatic but more final and I stepped up behind him, grabbed his bloody chin in one hand and slit his throat with the straight razor, pulling deep with the muscles of my shoulder and back until steel scraped across spine. He made a loud, "Huh!" from the opening in his neck and everyone went quiet.

Torture was one thing, but murder was a sin. That's why they needed me.

I pulled the trash bags from my pocket and the roll of tape and dumped his body to the floor. His fingers and toes came off with bolt cutters, made wet pops louder than you might expect. I heard some murmurs, more when I carried the pale digits to the oven and scattered them inside, turning the dial to 500 degrees. No one moved, though. No one left.

Theatrics.

Christina watched it all happening, and her eyes bulged over her gag when I crossed the kitchen to her with my dripping razor.

A show for her. For everyone in the room. For the city.

The aroma of pork roast was nauseatingly thick in the apartment by the time I set to work gift-wrapping the bodies in the plastic bags. Taking out the trash was part of the deal.

Spanish and Christina disappeared.

Word got out.

I got paid.

ELEVEN

I chewed Tylenol as Ava wound medical tape around my purpling ribs.

"Tighter."

"It'll hurt."

"I have two cracked ribs. They gotta be held in place. Pull it tighter."

I got through it without screaming, and she handed me a blue T-shirt. I hissed when I pulled it on and glanced down at the gold NYPD stamped over the breast.

"It was that or one with a big heart on it," Ava said.

"C'mere," he said.

I turned her around and pulled her hair back.

"Ow!" she said.

I slipped a rubber band on her ponytail and turned her to the mirror.

"I look trashy."

"Put on more of the cake, I can still see bruises."

She reluctantly picked up the makeup.

TWELVE

- 1 -

The cab disgorged us into the endless pick-and-roll of the crowd outside Grand Central Station. Massive stone edifice of a bygone age, hub of transit, sight of countless films and, these days, doing its best impression of a suburban mall with Manhattan pretensions. Though the skyscrapers around it tower over the station, it has a weight they lack, a stone idol squatting amidst saplings.

The madness of New York sidewalks has an order to it if you know how to ride the currents, but add in tourists and the flow goes to hell. Clusters of out-of-towners stopping to look at maps. To look up at the great stone structure. To pose in front of doors vomiting forth an endless stream of commuters who cursed and grumbled and pushed through. Foot traffic in every possible direction in the five-yard-width of cement sidewalks as engines rumbled, sirens wailed and people talked, talked and talked some more.

I led Ava west along Forty-Second Street and under the overpass, glancing back occasionally to offer a meaningless comment lost in the susurrus of noise, using the moments to scan our back trail and seeing nothing to raise my hackles. The intersection gridlocked when an ambitious Tomcat Bakery truck tried and failed to push across. I paused, not to help, just to watch, as a bent crone in a black hat and out-of-season winter coat brandished a cane in one knobby fist and tottered into the jagged maze of vehicles, trailing obscenities. "All right you motherfuckers, here I come."

We passed through a cloud of smoke at an aluminum-sided Halal cart and my stomach grumbled. My ribs answered back and I decided to wait on eating.

On Vanderbilt we headed north into a slightly diminished crowd where I kept myself within touching distance of the building, only taking Ava's hand when I hooked sharply and pushed through the doors, ignoring a businesswoman's muffled curse as we consumed precious seconds of her time.

The sound changed inside, countless footsteps and voices banging off the hard floor and walls as we lemminged between a Rite-Aid pharmacy and a small transportation museum. The smells of exhaust and smoke were replaced by sweat and a chemical mélange of body washes. Travelers deliberate in their movements flowed around pockets of look-ie-loos snapping pictures, reminiscing about *this* scene with *that* actor.

We entered the main terminal and Ava made a sound, looking at the high ceiling, at the great clock, ogling the bar and steakhouse up on the balcony level while I found the nearest electronic schedule and the Metro North train I wanted.

I picked a short line and she followed, saying something I ignored. I saw two cops and two more National Guardsmen in fatigues. Plainclothes were around but I hadn't made any yet.

A trio of septuagenarians stepped up to the ticket window. One started pulling papers out of a bag and piling them on the sill.

"Fuck," I said and grabbed Ava's wrist, pulling her in behind a stone-faced Hispanic lady with two children. I picked her because of the kids, quiet and attentive. She brooked no shit and transacted at the window quickly.

"Destination," said a bored lady with cornrows when I approached the window.

"Two for Albany."

"One way?"

"Round trip."

I slid her two twenties and she marked them with a pen, staring through big glasses that made her eyes enormous and round.

"All right, hon," she said, not bored, just tired. I thanked her and called her ma'am when I took the tickets and the change.

"Hungry?" I asked Ava and she nodded.

"How are your ribs?"

I grimaced and led her toward the wide, back staircase. There were more food options downstairs, but I liked the idea of high ground and we hit the west balcony and the Campbell Apartment.

Kind of place you'd take a date.

The doors were tall and the *maître d'* was short. He gave us a look that told me if it were crowded, we weren't getting in. But it was early.

The ceilings were high and the rugs oriental. Elegant chair sets surrounded low tables as if circling the wagons around important trade goods. Pale martinis with green olives. Red Manhattans in stemmed glasses big enough to mean something. It was a lounge plucked from Lucky Luciano's id, doing a hard sell with the Prohibition vibe but I didn't mind.

We took red seats at the end of a polished brown bar. Our view was a bounty of top-shelf booze interrupted by a narrow gent in a vest.

"What'll it be?"

"Bourbon, neat." I glanced at Ava who said, "The same."

"Any particular—"

I waved my hand and ignored the bolt of pain across my side. "Surprise us."

He smiled and slid sideways to the brown liquor.

"We going to Albany?" she asked.

I looked at the giant windows, maybe twenty feet high and half as wide, each one composed of grimy glass panes in squares of black metal. What I wanted were mirrors to see behind me so I turned, elbow on the bar. Captain Flirtatious. Violins played a concerto of complaint from my belt to my armpit, and beads of sweat debuted at my hairline.

"That's what the tickets say," I said, smiling, waiting for the goddamned drink.

Financial types making millions over gin. A few hotshots in open-collared shirts with sleek women in shoes so expensive they couldn't walk far. An old broad with the hair and jacket of a cozy mystery writer sat by herself at a nearby table and caught my eye, smiled. I nodded.

"Who tried to kill you?" Ava asked, and something horrible must have crossed my face because the old woman dropped her eyes as if she'd been darted. She picked up a drink in both hands and sipped.

"I walked into a door," I said to the old lady and turned back to find a beautiful brown pour in a cut glass. I could tell mine from Ava's because a shallow bowl of nuts separated the two drinks.

Smooth fire swelled behind my breastbone and I closed my eyes. Felt alternating waves of calm and anger.

"This place ain't the Holiday, but there ain't any Holidays within a couple blocks of Grand Central," I said and she nodded, sipping her drink. That was good advice so I finished mine and made a circle in the air for the bartender. He nodded and had the drinks back before the warmth evaporated from my mouth. At the Holiday I would've had to wake up the barman, hell, maybe give him CPR. I'd order a bottle if I wanted steady service.

"Some tycoon type in the 1920s built this place as his office and party spot. A salon, he called it. Filled it with Johnnies in creased suits and flappers with feathers in their hair. This whole city is like that. Old ghosts peeking at you through a crack in the blinds."

Sounds from the terminal were muted though there was a quiet vibration that spoke of trains. We could hear the murmur of the other patrons but it was like a private function at a museum. Words got lost in all the space and drifted apart.

"You come here a lot?" Bourbon softened her eyes.

"Not my kind of place," I said, but I'd been at the bar before, in a seat somewhere near the middle. Anger wormed up from my gut and I knocked back the rest of my drink, catching myself before I could crack it down on the gleaming wood. Old Slim would have the cops in through the door in two shakes and I needed to conserve ammunition.

I scooped a handful of nuts and shook them into my mouth, enjoying the salt. Two women alighted at the bar a seat away from Ava. Something about their hair and clothes said European, but their English was without accent. Geneva, I thought, but wasn't sure why.

"You've been here in New York a while, huh?" she asked.

I slid a fingertip around the damp rim of the glass and clocked a short man in a black suit sitting down on the other side of the European women. He touched his slicked-back hair and made a show for the ladies, opening his briefcase on the bar. *Good luck, pal.*

"It's hard to believe the place we spent last night and this," she jabbed her chin at the big room, "are in the same city. I always wanted to live here."

I pushed my empty glass away and reached for my silver.

"Well, now you're leaving."

- 2 -

The train ride north was uneventful.

- 3 -

She had two questions on the platform outside the Tarrytown station and neither of them was: Why aren't we in Albany?

"Can I bum a cigarette?" was her first question there on the platform, wind coming off the nearby Hudson River pushing her hair around her face. I pulled out the pack and shook one halfway out and she leaned over to take it with her teeth. When she stood, I flicked my Bic, both of us cupping our hands to protect the flame as she inhaled. I could hear the crackle of cigarette paper burning.

"Why did you bring me with you?" The words came out in a cloud of smoke, quickly tattered by another gust. She shivered and I remembered what she looked like the night before when all she had on was the invisible target I drew over her heart.

The train banged away from us and it occurred to me, not for the first time, that trains always sounded like broken machines, the way the metal crashed and clanged together. So, I said that thing and then, "Whoever is looking for me knows I work alone. Won't be looking for a happy couple."

The corners of her mouth stretched up and the tip of the cigarette danced when she said, "So let's go steal a car," and took my hand.

Always thinking about survival. Only thinking about survival.

We walked away from the shining expanse of the Hudson River, across the tracks and into the train station at Tarrytown, which some folks call Sleepy Hollow.

In the parking lot we stole a Chevy.

THIRTEEN

- 1 -

Plastic Jesus bobbled his head at me and I said, "You," to the figure stuck to the pebbled blue plastic of the dashboard.

"What?" Ava asked.

"Fucker's following me," I said. We were across the border in Vermont and had stopped in a shopping center parking lot. While she grabbed a sack of burgers, I stole a muddy New Hampshire license plate from a four-wheel-drive Subaru and put it on the Chevy. The shin of my pants was still wet from kneeling in a puddle.

The pain came back while I was waiting for her and I doled out a small bump of cocaine onto my knuckle, snorting quickly and coughing against the rancid drip down the back of my throat. I needed to distract myself from the pain so I started talking.

"Was in LA a few years back in an old Charger. You know, Dodge, big engine. Not mine. Owner had a bobblehead like this on the dashboard."

I trailed off then, fighting the cocaine urge to chatter. I picked up the soda cup from between my legs and sipped from the straw, heading southbound on Route 30 past a steady flow of summer traffic. The sun was bright and the sky blue overhead as we raced between rows of towering pines. We were in Green Mountain country, heading downhill.

I was sweating even with the window cracked. The air flowing in smelled of hot tar and drew a hard furrow through my short hair. The roof of my mouth was dry from the cocaine and I felt fidgety.

"See if you can get the air conditioning working," I told her and she reached to play with the dials, cheek full of hamburger, eyes on me.

"What?" I said, flicking my eyes her way. A truck rumbled past on the left and the Chevy shivered in its wake.

"What happened in Los Angeles?"

I told her.

- 2 -

Neatnick DeMarco sipped his coffee and felt the brandy kicker warm his belly, sinking back into the luxuriant back seat of the mint condition Oldsmobile 98 as Vin drove them northbound on La Cienega Boulevard. The seats were soft, velour colored like red wine, and contoured to his body after so many years. A horn snarked to his right and he glanced at the Porsche revving past. Sneered. Wannabes hurried. If you had it made you went slow. A gentleman's pace.

They passed the concrete monstrosity of the Beverly Center and saw the flashing lights of the Star Strip declaring NUDE GIRLS INSIDE. He grinned around yellow teeth, still his very own.

"Remember when we used to stop in there?" he said to the back of Vin's head, a curly-haired silhouette against the rainbow neon lights washing over the windshield. "Take the girls across the street to…" He trailed off, trying to see the place but they were already slowing for the light at Beverly Boulevard.

"Trashy Lingerie," Vin supplied from the front seat.

"Right, right. Trashy Lingerie," Neatnick said, holding his cup in both hands so he could take another sip. He hooked a gnarled finger in his tie and loosened it but didn't remove it. It wasn't classy to go out without a tie, even retired. "Buy 'em any kind of underwear they wanted and old Lou would sew it up right on the spot." He leaned forward and slapped a clawed old hand against the back of the front seat. "Right on the spot."

"Those were good days," Vin said. He'd been there.

"You were always a good boy," Neatnick said and Vin's head bobbed. The signal ticked steadily and he turned right when the flow of traffic allowed.

"You want we should go to La Dolce Vita?" Vin asked and Neatnick shook his head, sinking back into himself with a sigh.

"Nah, lets go home."

"You sure? I could call ahead and get it for takeout."

"Nah," Neatnick waved his hand, waiting until a stretch Hummer limousine blaring music rumbled past before continuing. "It ain't got the feel tonight."

"All right, boss," Vin said, flicking a look in the rearview, but the old man was only a shadow in the back seat. "I'll make you something at home."

Neatnick closed his eyes, feeling the warm wetness beneath the lids. It was twenty years since he retired. He thought some people would still call him "Mister" if he went anywhere, but lately all he wanted to do was drive around and look at things. Look at the offices on Sunset where he cut deals with the record guys. Pass Paramount Studios on Melrose Avenue where he had a piece of the Teamsters action. And the last time he went to Star Strip he felt nothing below the belt, even in the back room. When he invited a couple girls across the street for underwear, his treat, he saw pity in their eyes.

"Let's just go home," he said.

Vin accelerated left on La Brea Boulevard and snaked up into the Hollywood Hills where shadowy alcoves led to gated driveways. The houses didn't look like much from the road. One story, low and flat. But from the other side they were great, sprawling things, spilling for several stories down the hillside, gazing at the glittering spread of jewels below that was Los Angeles at night.

City of Angels. He sighed and coughed, wiping a cloth handkerchief against his wet lips. He was thinking of Chicago again. He'd never planned to return. The idea of living out the end of his life in the warmth and sunshine of LA was a dream to a kid from the South Side of the Windy City, but he just kept living on and on.

He carefully unscrewed the cap from the metal thermos at his side and listened to the liquid gurgle as he refilled his mug. Coffee with the sharp tang of alcohol beneath it.

He hadn't been back to Chicago since before he retired. Wasn't quite welcome. But thought maybe an old man might be allowed to walk the streets of his youth one last time.

Somewhere in there his eyes slid closed and the smooth purr of the engine lulled him into a doze. They opened again when the motion stopped. Saw black bars shining in the glare of their headlights.

"Vin?" he said, hating the worried old man sound he made.

"We're here," Vin said and the power locks thumped open in all four doors. They were new when the car rolled off the assembly line in 1968 and still worked like a charm. "Be right back. Gotta get the gate."

Neatnick smiled and sipped his coffee, glad he hadn't spilled it when he slipped off to sleep. Vin would be a minute. Thought the old man didn't know the boy was sneaking a smoke while opening the gate.

He pushed the liquid around his mouth with a wormy tongue.

Oh, he knew. He knew things all right. He—

The door beside him opened with a creak, and a black piece of night flowed into the back seat beside him. He inhaled to shout and swallowed coffee down the wrong pipe as the door closed. In the brief moment before the dome light went dim, he saw a face he didn't recognize. Dead eyes that ate the light.

He fumbled for the door handle to his left but felt a knuckle strike his temple. His hat tumbled free as white spots danced across his vision, and then two thick bars caught his neck in a vice grip, one against his spine and the other against his throat. A weight straddled him and he thought of lap dances at the Star Strip as his trachea was flattened beneath a powerful forearm.

Spit flapped from his lips and the killer leaned in close enough to kiss. Neatnick was struck with the notion that the man would bite his nose and he began to writhe desperately, but the grip didn't loosen and the eyes didn't move from a spot only inches in front of his.

Black eyes that ate the light. Dead eyes.

One hard wrench snapped the birdlike neck. The dome light barely had time to glow when the black form slipped out the door and closed it gently.

When Vin returned after the agreed upon time and found Neat-nick DeMarco dead he made a few calls and word got back.

Vin's sister was returned with nine fingers remaining.

- 3 -

Ava stretched out a finger and tapped Jesus on the head. "I got ketch-up on Jesus."

I snapped out of the zone, irritated at myself. Pain, lack of sleep and cocaine were making Jack a very dull boy.

Ava licked her finger clean and then wiped the plastic bobblehead free of offending condiments. "So why is he following you?"

"What?"

"Jesus."

I flicked a look at the bobbling head and thought *fuck you* thoughts. Came up with a story I could share.

"Because I'm a sinner."

"And what sin did you commit?"

She flashed a bullshit grin.

"All right," I said, shifting in my seat to get comfortable. "So I'm driving this Charger—"

"A friend's."

"Sort of a friend's," I said. "Anyway, it's loud, old school. Cruise through a parking garage and it sets off car alarms."

"I like it."

I flicked another look at her, scrunched into the corner of seat and door. I hit the lock button just to make sure she wouldn't tumble out onto the highway.

"So it's late and we're driving up La Cienega Boulevard. Friday night traffic. Music coming out of car windows."

"Who's we?"

"This girl."

"Ahhh."

"So I'm looking up to fix my mirror and when I look down her head is in my lap."

"Doing what?"

Ava had a great deadpan, I'll give her that.

"So she's doing what she's doing, and I'm having trouble concentrating—"

"In front of Plastic Jesus?"

"Right," I nodded. "He's watching and she's doing her thing and I'm driving slower and slower until I ease over into the right lane."

"And?"

"And I got stuck in a valet parking line behind a couple of BMW's outside, I think it was Nobu. Maybe Koi. One of those high-end restaurants."

Ava barked out a laugh and covered her mouth.

"So I'm sitting there right next to a crowd of people waiting for their rides while they smoked cigarettes, looking at this loud car, they can see her ass up in the air, head bobbing up and down."

Ava's shoulders were shaking and sounds escaped her fingers.

"And I'm trying to figure out what to do. It was a unique situation, right? And this valet looks at me, little guy in a red jacket, and gives me a thumbs up." I let out the laugh that had been building and she did too. It felt good even with the pain in my ribs.

"So now he's following you," Ava said, gesturing with her chin at bobblehead Jesus.

"Yes."

"Maybe hoping for a repeat performance?"

I shook my head. She slipped her lips over the straw and sucked, the rattle telling me her soda was mostly ice.

"Hey?" She wasn't smiling this time. "Are you a hitman?"

FOURTEEN

- 1 -

As our destination came into view I was surprised by a weight in my heart. I had a decision to make.

We stopped in Craxton, near Vermont's border with New Hampshire. My headlights picked out a blue road sign indicating hotel services and we exited, navigating through a small town center with brick and wood buildings before finding the hotel, a one-story building of white clapboards in the shape of an L. Eight units done in Bates Motel chic.

I pulled into the muddy, gravel lot, jouncing over potholes and expecting a comment about my driving or the hotel vibe. Ava's playful side. But she had gone quiet and stared out through her window.

"Stay here," I said and pushed out, cursing when I stepped in a mud slick. Mosquitoes lit on my exposed skin as I stepped up onto the cement sidewalk and scraped my shoes clean. Some kind of caged device was hung from the overhang, snapping and popping with blue electric flashes. I cursed the country before pushing through a moth-laden screen door and inside where the canned laughter of a TV show took a swing at loneliness.

The old lady behind the counter was eager for conversation but I was not, and finished a cash transaction brusquely enough that her plump face flushed with resentment.

"Night," I said and didn't wait for a reply.

When I stepped back into the bug-ridden night I saw Ava as an outline leaning against the hood of the Chevy, legs crossed at the ankle. I heard the scrape of a match and her face was lit orange from below, liquid eyes focused on my approach as she lit a fresh Parliament.

The match arced like a shooting star when she flicked it away and said, "So this is where you leave me, huh?"

- 2 -

I left her. Stood outside next to the car and heard a dog howling in the dark. Couldn't tell if it was inside my head or not.

I needed space. Time to think. To sober up. To figure out what was happening and what to do about it.

Ava.

I pulled open the door and a crust of dried mud crumbled to the ground. She was standing in the doorway to room number eight. Blue light from a TV flickered behind her and the edge of her silhouette became fluid.

The engine roared to life and she flinched away from the splash of headlights as I backed up and aimed toward town, a faint illumination over the trees in the near distance.

Instead, I pulled the Chevy around back and parked it out of sight from the road. I'd had the car for too long already and didn't want to play New Man in Town in a stolen ride. The lights played over the narrow bathroom windows at the back of the units, and I thought about how good a shower would feel.

Ava.

Walking. Mosquitoes landed in the streams of sweat trailing down my neck and I brushed them aside, crushing and crumpling bodies by the dozen. I smelled cinders and saw the beckoning stretch of train tracks behind the motel.

I traveled by starlight.

The ties were old but strong and I adopted a staggered march to match their length. The night was full of unaccustomed sounds. The crackle of twigs, the creaking of tree trunks. Far from quiet, it was alive with noise that would be missed beneath the clamor of cars and human speech.

I glanced up at a flutter to see what might have been bats. The sky between the stars was a richer color, somehow deeper than black, if that was possible. Alien.

I looked down at the rusting extent of the rails.

Grow up in the city and trains are like lifeblood. Subways and buses how you get around. But the real trains, trains that used tracks like I was following, held a promise of escape.

I had a gun and money. There was a Greyhound stop in town. Why I picked the place. I'd get to Boston and talk to Grace, see what the jungle drums were singing. How big this thing was. My trouble.

A weird rattling sound that I knew came from a throat, but maybe not human. I looked into the brush beside the tracks and saw green eyes. I slapped at a mosquito on my arm and the eyes vanished.

"Shit." My cigarettes were in the car.

The glow was visible for a little while before I realized the tracks were taking me toward it. A shimmering, shape-changing thing and what I thought were house lights resolved into a bonfire. As if labeling the thing made it real, I caught the scent of wood smoke, beckoning me.

I succumbed.

The buzz of voices rose in volume and separated into conversations, maybe two dozen people around the bonfire talking, drinking, smoking. Two people were slow dancing, and a woman plucked guitar strings off by herself, sitting on a fallen tree.

"Hey brother," a man said, burly and bearded, teeth visible in a smile.

"I saw the fire."

"The beacon, man," he said, clapping a paw on my shoulder. I allowed myself to be guided into the group. "Like the beacon of Amon Din." Off my look. "The beacons of Minas Tirith. *Lord of the Rings*, man!"

"Strider!" a blonde woman called out, straight hair swinging behind her down to her belt. These strangers welcoming me like a long-lost pal. Expecting me.

"Right?" my guide said. "He came out of the woods just like the Dunedain."

"Totally," she agreed.

I had no fucking idea what they were saying, but someone slapped a warm bottle of beer in my hand and I didn't complain as a few more of them gathered around. Even the guitar responded to my arrival with a flamenco lick.

I saw a kilt and T-shirts, not much shaving on the men and long tresses on most of the women, though a few sported short, punky hair.

I almost spit out the sip when the warm liquid hit my lips. Some kind of swamp water concoction. My welcomer laughed and said, "It's magic potion," pointing at a big metal pot balanced on rocks beside the fire. A woman crouched in front of it, dipping a beer bottle into liquid. Limned against the blaze she appeared naked.

"I'm Rick," my guide said, and I said, "Me too," and we laughed at the coincidence. I could smell the spices now. Cinnamon. Sage. Other things I recognized but couldn't name.

"C'mon," the blonde said, looping an arm through mine. I took another swig of the magic potion as she led me to a couple of stripped logs dragged into a V. "This is Rick," she said and greetings floated up to meet me as a stringy man in a leather vest with no shirt rose, offering a calloused hand.

"Dekkard," he said.

"Like *Blade Runner*," I said. The blonde nodded though she apparently carried no movie affiliation or name of her own.

Bottles were clinked and emptied. Mine was taken and a freshly filled replacement found my palm. Eyes glittered in the firelight and a joint was passed around. Someone gave me their last cigarette, half smoked. I wreathed my head in a grey cloud and watched a couple who sat in the dirt while investigating a length of beads as if unraveling a secret code.

Stars overhead became streaks of light across the dome of the sky.

People came and went. I heard the high whine of dirt-bike engines and saw headlights flashing down a forest path. There was music and talk. I remember words like Rivendell and replicant and when asked about the tragedy of Roy Batty I responded, "Kill 'em all." Which set off a new round of debate but was apparently not wrong.

Dekkard leaned in to whisper through a visible cloud of rank breath, "You a cop?" When I shook my head he asked, "You sure?" And I saw that his eyes glittered with rat-like intelligence. I shook my head and looked for my jacket, saw the blonde was wearing it though she'd apparently lost her T-shirt somewhere.

Rick gave me another bottle of potion and called me, "Name brother." I grinned like I understood. Two women with short hair danced with a guy in slacks and a white shirt, his tie wrapped around his slick-backed hair like a bandana. They waved me over but I stayed where I was.

Spirals of light trailing down from above. I tried to explain it to the blonde as she kissed my neck, pointing with my finger and noticing how the sky dimpled at my touch, Christmas lights blurring and sliding toward my fingernail.

Music filled my ears and I heard someone say, "Lady of the fuckin' Wood." I looked at the roving guitar player as she plucked something uptempo and sang liquid sounds that I enjoyed but made no sense.

I was the last one to notice her circling the fire, arms like sinuous serpents. Her long mass of hair swung out as if she were twirling quickly, but it had to be slow motion because I could pick out every detail of Ava's face. Even when she spun away her eyes stayed locked on mine.

I went to her and took her hand, twirling. Floating. Our feet barely grazed the earth. Bodies moved around us, everyone dancing. Clothes falling away. Someone had turned on a boom box and music filled the air.

It was like something out of a movie. A sex-drenched dream. The party descending into orgiastic psychedelia.

Then there were knives.

- 3 -

Ava's face drifted to mine and our lips grazed when I felt hands on either shoulder and we were separated, the two women with short hair guiding me backwards.

"Hey," I said and my voice came from far away. I wanted to laugh at how ridiculous I sounded but saw the guy with the tie wrapped around his head say something to Rick who wrapped big arms around Ava and turned her away. I realized she was struggling.

"Hold still, big boy," the woman on my right said, and her partner on my left twisted my wrist in a cop's hammer lock. All around me the revelers were circling, eyes huge and stoned in the flickering light, slack-jawed and grinning with wood and steel clutched in eager fists. Primitive by firelight. Humanity's oldest self showing through.

A shard of silver glowed in the dark and I saw the knife in Dekkard's hand. Grunted through the pain and torqued my left wrist, stomping with my left foot as I twisted and shoved, and the woman on that side lurched into Dekkard. I saw steel sprout from her back and Dekkard looked as if had been slapped awake.

My movements felt strange and elongated, hands telescoping out too far from my arms, my feet stretching miles below to find the ground. Eyes swam toward me. Teeth.

I felt a tug from my right side and grabbed the woman's face with my left hand, digging a finger into a nostril, fish-hooking the corner of her mouth. She tried to bite and hang on but I yanked her around and freed my right hand.

The Beretta appeared like magic and I shot her in the back of the head, spreading her face over the campground.

Another gun fired, the sound higher pitched, and a reveler toppled into the fire. Running. Screaming. I saw bearded Rick grappling with someone, and when they separated the man with the slicked-back hair and tie worn like a bandana put two rounds from a compact pistol into Rick's chest.

I remembered the guy then, from the Campbell Apartment. His show of hitting on the European women. Not a performance for them, but for me. Hiding in plain sight.

This one was a pro.

I jerked off a round but hurried the shot and missed. He dropped to one knee and fire blossomed at the end of his gun. Wind creased my cheek. Someone hit me in the knees and I fell, clubbing Dekkard in the temple with the butt of my Beretta until I jammed the barrel against his shoulder and squeezed the trigger. He released a coyote's cry of pain and rolled away but my next bullet blew out his heart.

My friend from the Apartment was still on one knee, slapping a short magazine into the pistol, low capacity being a problem with some compact weapons. He snicked back the slide and looked up into deadly black eye of the 9mm. I put a round through his collarbone. He shrieked, clawing at the wound as I cursed and lumbered closer, my aim gone to hell. I stomped on his ankle, and when he curled in on it to protect himself, I dropped a knee on his ribs and shoved the pistol in his ear. Crushed the trigger.

His head deflated, brains slapped out in a fan shape on the ground. People were crying around us. Dying. Others running. The boom box was on its back but still offering a soundtrack for the bloody show.

"Ava?"

I whirled around in a circle, a crazy man spinning by firelight as I tried to reassemble my brain. I saw the blonde then, breasts flattened by gravity where she lay on her back, eyes wide in death.

She was still wearing my jacket and that seemed important, but I didn't know why.

"Ava?" I staggered toward people writhing in the dirt but didn't see her.

"You fucker," someone spat and I shook my head, couldn't find Ava anywhere.

Wailing that might have come from a human throat or police siren. I rubbed my eyes. Scraped at my ears.

"Fucker!" someone shouted again, and I backed away from the carnage. My feet caught on the railroad ties as I escaped through the woods.

- 4 -

She wasn't in the room.

I cursed, my thoughts trapped like a fly in tree sap. What did I owe her? Where did she go? I was banging around like a fool, making noise. I tipped over the chair as if she would be hiding beneath it.

I heard more sirens and heard my own voice say, "Time to go."

And I was in the parking lot, the room's door hanging open in my wake. My shoes pounded on gravel and splashed through mud, and then I was sliding into the driver's seat. Too late, I saw the passenger window was broken.

I reached for my gun but her hand stayed my arm and her lips brushed my ear.

"Drive," she said.

I did.

The road wound between the trees and I drove with Ava's hand on my arm, windows down to cool us off and clear our heads, rushing air fat with the smell of evergreens.

We passed a burning building on the way out of Craxton. A big one. All the king's horses and all the king's men were invited, and no one had time to notice our little bullet party in the woods. My assassin creating a distraction to draw law enforcement. Thinking things through, right up until I killed him.

We crossed the state line into New Hampshire and arrived at a village named Burton and a motel called The Pines. Ava didn't argue when I told her to stay in the room and was watching TV in the dark when I left. A mile down the road I saw a light. The bar was called Mellow Mary and leaked music the way dead Dekkard leaked blood. I left the car there, planning to be long gone before anyone asked questions.

The walk back was long enough for me to realize the depth of my trouble. Not just in New York, but following me. A bounty on my head. Campbell Apartment felt like Mafia. Yakuza in the park. Little Odessa blew up my room at The Quiet Man.

Death coming from all directions and me falling apart. The heels of my hands were pressed against my temples, holding my head together as I walked. I needed clarity.

I would sober up. Plan. Survive.

My mouth was cotton dry when I dragged into the parking lot of The Pines and I wondered if she had waited. Realized that I cared about the answer.

My eyes adjusted to the blue moonlight streaming in through the motel room window, illuminating Ava with her back to me, bare skin glowing silver. She swayed aside to reveal that she was clutching the bed frame.

I moved up behind her and saw that I was holding my lighter. I needed to understand.

"I want to read them."

"Only the cursed can read them," she said but held still, eyes holding my face as I rolled the flint and a flame appeared. I saw beads of perspiration on the underside of her right breast and lifted it with my free hand, bringing the flame close enough to see the twisting strand of black ink.

I met her gaze, holding the flame close but not touching as she breathed through her nose. "I can't read it," I said, letting the flame die. She let a sigh escape and shook her head.

Then: "Take off your shirt."

I peeled off the shirt and my ribs cried out like a voice from another room. The holstered Beretta clunked down on the small night table.

"Do you want this?" she whispered.

Sweat beaded on my face and torso. A window fan was pushing the air around the room but did nothing to lessen the heat.

"Yes," I said.

A sigh, almost a moan, and I pressed into her back, reaching around, running my hands over her breasts, her thighs. I lowered my head and read her curses with my tongue. Bit the mandalas that tipped her.

She arched into me as I fumbled with my belt.

"Do it," she growled.

I buried my face in her hair and her chin rose. My teeth found her neck.

- 5 -

Sunlight streamed in through the windows and dust motes danced in the air.

I rested, aware of the sweat pooling on my abdomen, the tangled moisture at my groin. Air currents from the fan tickled. My head was clear and it felt good not to wake up with a hangover.

Magic potion indeed.

Had last night happened? I blinked and tried to sort out the last twelve hours. Another curse was written over our bed in Ava's blood. Her breathing changed and I knew she was awake. After a minute of listening to her, hearing the faint whistle of air through a gap in her front teeth, I spoke.

"Who do you want me to kill?"

- 6 -

The good feeling stayed with me as I browsed the racks at a Cumberland Farms in town and bought a cheap cell phone along with two large coffees. A bell tinkled when I backed out through the door before handing one cup to Ava while I set mine on a bench and powered up the phone.

"I'll just be a minute," I said and watched Ava's sway as she ambled to our car and climbed inside.

The coffee smelled inviting and my mood was light until a chime announced that the phone was alive. I activated the web browser and waited for the slow connection, planning to email Grace and set a time to talk on the phone if she hadn't left word for me.

Bonfire by the tracks

There it was, the message waiting for me amidst the hotel deals and offers of an online education. Beads of sweat along my hairline grew clammy, and I turned the phone to locate the volume button, tapping it until it was as loud as it would go. A touch of my thumb played the video file attached to the email.

The footage was shaky and bad, dark shapes on screen swirling around the blinding glare of the bonfire. "Hey boys, the Rooster was almost roasted by a real wild crew in Vermont," the familiar voice shared, my very own Hanoi Hannah gleeful even through the molasses quality of distortion. "But you know how it goes, they missed and he rolled." The blur of motion clarified into violence and I saw an image of myself shoving two people off me. The flare of a muzzle flash and one of them went down.

The footage bounced crazily over the ground as whoever shot the film ran from the fight. "That's right boys, the Rooster is alive and heading east. Who's gonna claim the prize? Who's it gonna be?"

The video ended and I played it again, hunching lower and shading the screen to watch it a second time.

I deleted the message and pulled up the phone function to call Grace. She answered on the first ring like she was out of breath.

"Get out," Grace said like she thought I was still in New York.

"What?" I said, straining to hear over the whistling of a bad connection. I squinted at our car but couldn't see Ava through the blinding glare off the windshield.

"They're coming for you."

"Who?"

"Everyone."

I heard a click and the call went dead. I destroyed the phone with a sharp crack and threw it in the nearby trashcan, backing away as if the phone might lunge forth like a snake.

"Excuse me," a voice said and I stopped, muttering apologies as a young woman carrying plastic bags full of soda bottles pushed by on the sidewalk. The door to the store opened with a tinkle and she went inside. Returnables, maybe.

The day was hot and insects buzzed from a nearby field as cars passed leisurely on the two-lane road. The sky was blue with only a few white clouds. I tried to stare up past the atmosphere into the black of space where a careening metal satellite might be staring down at me that very second. I felt like a cockroach in the middle of the kitchen floor when a light goes on. Like a bug on slide, all my secrets revealed.

Who's gonna claim the prize? Who's it gonna be?

I studied a middle-aged man as he emerged from a pickup truck and adjusted his pants before heading for the store. Was his face familiar? Had he followed me from New York?

They're coming for you.

What the hell was going on?

FIFTEEN

- 1 -

Boston is a city built for murder.

I know. I've dumped almost as many bodies into the muddy flow of the Charles River as I have in the Hudson and East River combined.

It's a city of knuckles and Irish resentment. Somewhere along the way too much blood was spilled and it seeped into the bricks, watering the sidewalks with violence. The glittering jewel of downtown, of the Hancock Building and the monolithic Financial District, these places are not the city. Tourists crawling like maggots over the waterfront or the historic Freedom Trail never saw past the mask and powdered wig Boston pulls over its snarling face.

My boots crunched over shards of green glass as a lowered Chevy Caprice with custom rims rolled past. White kids leaking dead stares from acne-scarred faces eye-fucked me while a bass beat fuzzed their subwoofers, rattling glass windows in the chipped frames of narrow row houses. People on porches with beer cans in their fists and cigarettes in their mouths ignored the car, kept their eyes on me.

The stranger.

The street bent sharply and angled down past Chester Avenue and Watts, a bitch in the winter but just a hassle in the hot summer. It smelled like the sea, rotting and enticing. I was deep in the rabbit's warren of Chelsea, which clung to its larger neighbor like a barnacle on the hull of a ship.

Boston, city of killers.

I wanted a bank robber.

- 2 -

From the outside it didn't look like much, a clapboard single-story building painted barn red, long since brutalized into a chipped and faded grey by decades of New England weather. A round window sprouted like an eye beside the wooden door and boasted a Schlitz sign. Someone making a point about the lack of art classes in Boston's public school system had painted SULLY's over the door. Not even Mother Theresa would call that scrawl calligraphy.

Inside you realized the outside was the best part of the deal. It was dark and the plank floor was uneven and eager to trip. Low lightning revealed a long bar fronted with countless Bruins stickers, the endless black and yellow blurring into a long visual insult. It smelled like sour beer with a frisson of industrial cleaner. The perfume of unwelcome.

Three guys inside when I walked in, one short man seated at the bar flinching away from the intrusion of sunlight. Another short guy in a beat-up denim jacket was in the corner, shaved head bent low over a tabletop Ms. Pac-Man, muffled *beeps* and *boops* blending with the hiss of AM sports radio.

The third short guy was behind the bar, oldest of the bunch, reading a Stephen King paperback and periodically stroking his combover. He dog-eared a page and looked up when I sat on a stool, watching as I stood back up and chose another, steadier model.

"Yah?" he asked.

"Bud."

He turned away and placed a glass beneath the three-handled draft station. A fresh, cool smell rose as he filled the glass and slid it too me.

"Three bucks."

I slipped him a five and nodded. He rapped his knuckles on the bar and opened an old black register. A bell rang when he banged it shut.

I sipped, eyeing the wet ring on the unfinished bar surface as the slight spillage irrigated some letters carved into the wood. JT Sux Cock.

There was a flurry of movement as Ms. Pac-Man strode across the room with his fists balled into his jacket pockets. He shot me a look from the door and said, "Yankees suck," before letting it bang shut behind him.

"So does his mother," the bartender said, and I nodded at the irrefutable wisdom. The first short guy remained at his end of the bar, hands clasped before him as if in prayer, forehead on his fists. Maybe snoring.

I was listening to a furniture commercial in which two enthusiastic brothers shouted over each other when I heard the door creak open and tossed a glance over my shoulder. The newcomer ducked his head when he came inside, tall enough to play basketball, ginger mop brushing the mantle. He was a gangly, uncoordinated looking man, all bones and angles with fingers like pale bananas. His jeans were stained and he wore a grey sweatshirt in spite of the heat.

He took a moment before releasing a sigh and clomping up beside me. He grabbed a stool, felt the wobble, and moved around to the other side where things were sturdier.

"Sean," I said. He scratched filthy fingernails against his cheek and I wondered if he was rebuilding an engine. The bartender moseyed around the bar and out the door, "I'm out for a smoke."

"Hey, John," he said and I nodded. I was John Gallo in Boston. "Why you here?"

"Here for you, Sean."

"Fuck, why?"

"Let's talk in private."

He was facing the bottles behind the bar but I knew his eyes were sliding over to check me out. Deciding if he could say something.

"Funny you should show up now," he said.

"Why?"

"C'mon," he said and pushed back. His bar stool clattered to the floor.

- 3 -

Sean needed a favor.

"I know it's like asking Yves St. Laurent to sew up the ass of my jeans."

"Who?" I asked.

"The fashion designer."

I looked at his ratty sweatshirt and let it go, bending low out of the wind to light a cigarette.

The Pontiac didn't look like much but the rumble under the hood meant business. There was no air conditioning so we had the windows down, elbows out as we crossed the Chelsea Street Bridge. The dashboard was sticky to the touch, and there were greasy wrappers crumpled in the footwell, but when I asked for a working car, Sean chose the Pontiac.

The wind played with my hair.

In the back seat was a heavy-browed kid with his blond hair shaved down to stubble. He had a Roman numeral IV tattooed on the side of his neck and wore scabs on his knuckles.

"My sister's kid," Sean explained when he saw my expression.

"I'm—" Number Four had opened his mouth to say something but Sean jabbed a long finger in his face and said, "Shut up. You don't talk to him. Don't say a fuckin' word."

"He owes these Israeli assholes fifteen large," Sean explained to me. "They fronted a deal with this nigga and the fucka ripped him off." Sean looked like he wanted to beat his nephew to death right there inside the Pontiac, this part happening when we went to pick the kid up. "Fuckin' Jews are gettin' uptight, gettin' ready to send him a message for takin' so long to pay 'em back. He's hustlin' maybe a grand a week but they say it ain't enough."

Sean couldn't go to his crew, professional thieves who wanted nothing to do with the drug trade.

I punched the radio button with a knuckle. AC/DC laid down cruel guitar riffs while Bon Scott howled about being on a highway to Hell.

"Where is this place?" I asked.

- 4 -

I could taste Gloucester in the salt on my tongue. A decaying sea stink that inflated my nostrils, enervated my blood, tickling something deep inside the monkey brain.

The sky was filled with gulls wheeling over wooden piers that thrust themselves out into the Atlantic, splattered white with guano and grey with dried fish scales. Working docks, not tourist attractions. The sounds were pervasive. Screaming birds and shouting men. A constant rustle of waves. Our engine was an unwelcome intrusion and Sean turned the ignition key, shutting down, letting the ocean sounds in.

I took a Phillips-head screwdriver and a pair of pliers from the glovebox and slapped it closed with a hollow whack. The tools went into a pocket and Sean shot me a look. I shrugged.

Men in stained overalls catcalled as a fishing boat chugged closer, pushing up a foaming white bow wave. A dolly with plastic trays was wheeled to the end of the dock.

"You know being a commercial fisherman is more dangerous than being a cop?" Sean said and I shook my head. "Only thing worse is being a lumberjack."

The gangly redhead threw an arm over the seatback and glared at his nephew. "Where are the muthafuckas?"

"They got a boat," Number Four said.

"A fuckin' boat?" Sean shook his head. "How'd you meet these assholes?"

"Fuckin' Ritchie," Number Four said.

"Fuckin' Ritchie," Sean said. He nodded, psyching himself up. "You got what you need?"

I pushed open my door, unfolding my legs into the onshore breeze. Breathed it in through my nose. The sky was blue and the water was green. If we had to dump a body, we couldn't throw it in the ocean. The current would wash it onto a beach. We'd have to go inland a half mile or so, weight it down and stick it in the weedy part of a salt marsh. Let the crabs at it.

"You got the money?" I asked Number Four. He slapped a bulge in his front pocket.

"Give," I said, and he froze until Sean nodded. Number Four pulled out a Ziploc bag holding a wad of cash and I stuffed it inside my jacket.

Sean was looking around, watching the fishermen, checking out a handwritten sign. "Should grab some littlenecks before we leave," he said. "Two bucks for a dozen clams is pretty good."

"Show me this boat," I told Number Four, and the blocky kid set off past a forklift, his sloped shoulders rolling with his gait. I lifted and dropped my own shoulders a couple of times and shook my fingers out. Felt my breath trying to quicken and concentrated on tasting the air in long, slow sweeps as I dragged it in.

This kind of unplanned action was stupid. Was why so many guys did time. But I was in a bind and needed Sean's help.

"There it is," Number Four pointed at a charter fishing boat tied up at the dock. It was clean and I couldn't see any fishing equipment on deck. Not running charters at the moment.

It bobbed on a wave and I saw the gold calligraphy at the bow.

Ava's curses by fire light.

Read the name Tequila Sunrise.

So, they were assholes.

"How many onboard?" I asked.

"Two, sometimes four guys," Number Four said. "Kid I know is Jamie."

Sean looked embarrassed, but I ignored him and crouched beside a stack of stinking wood pallets. I slipped the Beretta from my shoulder holster and threaded the silencer onto the barrel. Racked the slide and chambered a round.

"Hey—" Number Four said but blanched when my eyes found his.

"Don't let anybody on or off the boat," I growled and walked swiftly out onto the dock, picking up a smooth reggae sound as I drew closer to the Tequila Sunrise, my arm held straight down at my side, pistol along my thigh.

The tide was gentle and the boat pushed rhythmically against the wooden dock, a row of rubber tires absorbing the shock. I looked through the pilothouse windows and saw nothing so I timed the roll and hopped lightly onboard, moving right to the rear of the pilothouse as if I belonged.

The hatch was open, a cramped stairway descending into dim blue light. I smelled garlic and marijuana.

I followed my Beretta down the stairs, careful not to slip and make an embarrassing entrance. The stink of weed was choking, and I ducked my head to enter a smoke-filled dining area. Three young guys sat around an open pizza box on a wooden table.

"What?" a curly-haired kid said, chrome lighter in one hand and orange-tinted glass bong in the other. I backhanded him across the brow with the gun barrel and a sheet of red washed down over his eyes. I snatched a snub-nosed .38 from the table before the other two realized they were in trouble. One dropped a slice of pizza back into the box and the other braced his hands as if to stand.

I shot the CD player in the corner, and they recoiled from the metallic whack of the slide and the plastic crack of the music machine shattering.

"Shit!" About-to-Rise said and I leveled the pistol at his nose while Bong Boy shrieked and the Pizza Eater coughed, choking.

"Which one of you fucks is Jamie?" I asked.

The coughing lad pounded a fist against his chest and jerked a thumb at About-to-Rise, who shot him a curdled look.

"Who are you?" Jamie asked and I yanked the screwdriver from my pocket, slamming it down like an ice pick through the top of his hand until the tip bit into the wood. I jammed the silencer into his eye and his jaw dropped, mouth open.

"Scream and I kill you," I said and an awful wheeze escaped him. I left his hand pinned to the table and fished the baggy full of cash from my pocket, held it beneath the light hanging over the table.

"Here's the payment for this week," I said, dropping the money on the table. Tiny rivers of red reached across the table toward the parcel. I shuffled my feet with a sharp roll of the boat and continued, "Mark is going to keep paying every week, what he can afford because he owes you. It's your money."

"You're with Marky?" Jamie said and stared at me. The light swayed, throwing shadows back and forth across the cramped cabin, the wake of the incoming trawler shaking things up.

"If he gets hurt in the meantime, if he so much as stubs his toe, I will kill all three of you, understand?"

Jamie was pawing at his injured hand, and I pounded the pistol butt against the screwdriver. He squealed but slapped a palm over his mouth.

"When he's paid off, you never do business with him again." I drew out the pliers. I brought them down hard and caught Jamie's trapped ring finger, squeezed my hand into a white-knuckled fist around the handles. All three of them flinched from the wet pop of the finger bone. The color abruptly left Jamie's face and he slumped, eyes at half-mast.

"I have to come back, I'll do that to your fuckin' prick. Got it?"

"Yessir," the kid I'd pistol-whipped said, one hand pressed to the gash on his scalp, the other holding the forgotten bong.

I backed away, feeling for the lip of the hatch with my heel, and stepped through with the gun swaying back and forth between all three of them.

When my heel touched the stairs, I turned and ascended quickly and was on deck in moments.

I dropped the .38 in the water as I hopped across the open space to the dock.

"We good?" Sean asked as I met them on solid ground. I nodded and he stabbed a finger into his nephew's shoulder. "Say thank you."

Number Four looked at his shoes and said, "Thanks."

I squinted against the bright reflections off the rear windows in front of us as we ground south through traffic on Route 128 toward the city. We kept trying to roll up the windows against the choking atmosphere of exhaust and melting tar but would give up after a stifling minute or two. We were just cranking everything back open again when Sean said, "We forgot the littlenecks."

SIXTEEN

- 1 -

Waves flashed and sparkled in the summer sun, and a steady sea breeze cooled me as I stood near the bow of the water taxi, enjoying the ocean spray.

Boston Harbor has a thick smell, more potent than New York's harbor. The rush of wind and thrum of the boat's engine was cut only by the sound of the seagulls orbiting overhead.

Lost among the tourists lining the railing, I lifted the binoculars to my eyes and played them across the luxuriant waterfront properties until I located a seven-story wood-and-glass building at the end of Battery Wharf. I wore a Red Sox windbreaker that rippled in the breeze, and a small duffel bag at my feet contained my somewhat worse for wear black suit and the 9mm Beretta.

A fishing trawler trundled past on the port side and the tourists rushed away from where I stood, cameras snapping, one woman narrating a video.

Why the fuck do people do that? Go someplace and miss seeing it so they can watch a recording later. Maybe that was the difference between my kind and square Johns. Living life instead of recording it.

I tracked the binoculars along the top floor until I found the window I wanted and adjusted the focus, but the polarized glass defeated my attempts to see inside.

The view blurred as I lowered my aim and twisted the focus knob to reveal a low, three-story structure at the end of the next wharf. It was designed like a block of dark, hard wood and had been around in one incarnation or another since the turn of the eighteenth century. Officer barracks. Speakeasy. Restaurant. Now it was a private club. That's where she'd be. My Grace.

"Excuse me, but would you mind taking our picture?"

The woman was short and middle-aged, somewhere southern from her sound. He wore a polo shirt tucked into shorts and a phone clipped to his belt. His lipless mouth grinned beneath a bushy mustache.

"Sure, right here?" I asked, taking the camera and indicating the button. When she said yes, I waited for them to link arms at the railing and said, "Go Yankees." I snapped the picture while their faces contorted and held out the camera until the man reached for it.

The sun was hot on my scalp as I ambled back toward the stern, wondering how much I could trust Grace. The plant on her balcony was where it was supposed to be, on the right side. Did that mean that she got my message and all was well? Or she was inside the condo with her throat cut while a couple of goons endured the mounting stink, waiting for my arrival.

Had she sold me out entirely?

I fished a cigarette from the pack and tried to light it in the wind, ignoring the No Smoking signs posted all over the boat. But the Atlantic kept exhaling against me and I gave up after a few tries, flicking the cigarette into the foaming wake.

A seagull dove after my coffin nail.

- 2 -

As she ran blunt fingers over my face, I wondered how many diapers she'd changed, how many sore muscles she'd rubbed with liniment, and feet she'd massaged after a long day on the assembly line. She touched my face like a workman approaching a new job, the way Sean touched a car engine.

"Too thin," the old woman said. "Sit here," she ordered, pulling out one of the mismatched chairs from around the table in the kitchen. Number Four carried in a long, dark board that acted as a table extender, and Sean clomped onto the linoleum floor with an extra chair in each hand. "We usually save that seat for David, but tonight it's for you," she added.

I had no idea who David was and had only met the woman a half hour before when Sean led me into the low, weathered house with scalloped aluminum fronting over the porch. Inside the floors were dressed in thin rugs, and the walls wore ornate paper faded to yellow after fifty years of family life, but the real personality of the place was in the smell, something flatulent, organic and somehow appetizing. A great metal pot was boiling on the stove in the kitchen and the room sweated with fragrant steam. A sloppy yellow dog of unknown make forced his way under the table and added his bark to the family din, seemingly unable to shift position without bumping into my knees.

The woman's name was Annabelle and she didn't want to know anything about her grandson's work, only that I had helped him solve a big problem with "those people."

Number Four was her pride and joy, but she sat me at the head of the table. I rested my elbows on the plastic place mat and absently twirled the lazy Susan, causing salt and pepper shakers in the form of matching snowmen to clink together.

It was surreal, several family members coming and going at all times, conversations shouted from one room to the next or up the stairs with Annabelle at the center of it all. Cousins. Siblings. They folded me right into the mix like I came by every Sunday for dinner.

"Beer?" Sean asked, digging in the fridge.

I shook my head. Said, "Just a Coke if you got one," when I realized he hadn't seen me. A wet tongue licked the hand resting in my lap, and I jumped as Sean gave me an RC Cola. I popped the can, carbonated fizz tickling my nostrils as I held it in front of my mouth, waiting for it to simmer down before drinking.

"You should have a Coke, Sean," Annabelle said, wiping her hands on the blue, patterned housedress she wore and flicking her fingers into his shoulder. "You boys drink too much."

Sean slugged down half of his bear and belched. Number Four laughed as Annabelle shook her head. A kid named Kevin, maybe ten, giggled madly and said something about, "TV in the front room!" The noise level rose as the front door squeaked open and I heard feet on the staircase headed up. Sean's cousin Lisa stuck her head through the doorway, purple fingernails appearing as she braced her hands on either side.

"She's goin' upstairs to change." Blonde hair was tied off in a ponytail and she had the freshly scrubbed look of a woman who'd just washed off her makeup.

"What the fuck, Lisa?" Sean blurted, swallowing beer. "You were gone foreva."

"Fuck you, Sean." Lisa's bleached bangs flopped over her eyes and she blew them aside. "I took her to my friend Jean on Newbury and she sent us over to Bahney's after."

"Bahney's?"

"Bahney's."

"What's Bahney's?" I interjected.

"Expensive," Sean answered.

I was irritated that Ava had gone upstairs without stopping in and annoyed that I was irritated about it. I rubbed my temples and wished the cola were a beer.

Fuck that, a whiskey.

"Barney's is very nice," Annabelle added, reinserting the R that eluded most New Englanders. She carefully set a plate swimming with juices down before me, mounds of pink ham, white mashed potatoes and pale green cabbage mixed with orange carrots rising like islands in a miniature sea. I picked a yellow hair off the liquid and Annabelle cursed, "That damned dog," even as she bent low and held a chunk of ham under the table.

"Dig in, don't wait," Sean said and pushed back his chair to help Annabelle hand out more plates. I set down my soda and picked up the fork, stabbing a piece of ham and bringing it to my mouth where it broke apart like a wave on the rocks of my teeth. I closed my eyes, stunned at the flavors, at the aroma of ham and broth coating my palate and rising up to my nose.

"You like?" I opened my eyes to see Annabelle's face only inches from my own, and I smiled around the mouthful, only aware just then that I probably should have cut the piece.

"He likes," Sean said and sat down with his own plate, immediately committing a cardinal sin by squeezing yellow mustard over everything that dared to poke above the broth.

I scooped up dripping strands of limp cabbage and chewed, noting the source of the slightly unpleasant yet appealing smell as I swallowed them down and scooped up a heaping forkful of mash as a chaser. I cut off a small piece of ham and surreptitiously slid it under the table, expecting I'd wince but surprised at the gentle brush of lips and hard teeth as the morsel was plucked away.

"Annabelle, you've outdone yourself." Sean said as Number Four passed me a basket of warm rolls, the kind that came from a can. I slathered butter on one and soaked up some broth, trying not to down it all in one bite, complaints of my headache and damaged ribs fading to background din as my stomach and taste buds took over the controls of my brain.

When was the last time I ate food like this? In a setting like this? I felt a rush of affection for the people around me before hearing the mystical tread of the black dog slinking in, raising his muzzle to howl in my ear, a howl of anguish so loud I was shocked no one at the table heard it. That they weren't fleeing in a clatter of dropped plates and tipped chairs as the swirl of painful noise erupted from me.

The yellow dog shoved his snout into my crotch and made some kind of yawning sound. I met his upturned eyes and knew he heard my howling.

Sean was studying me and an internal governor slipped out of gear as I prepared to surrender. Opened my mouth to ask for a beer, ten beers, a bottle of whatever he had that was a brown. A line of cocaine, a snort of heroin or meth to blow the fucking black dog back into the corner...

Ava entered the room and my breath stopped.

Her mass of dark curls was pulled back into a simple chignon at the back of her head, so dark that it glinted a lustrous blue. The make-up was different, subtle, her eyebrows narrower and arched and her dress long and black, leaving her arms bare so that for the first time I noticed the line of muscle in her shoulders. The collar was high in what I was later told was *mandarin* and the dress ended at her knees. My eyes traveled down the burnished caramel of her shins to see she wore low black heels of a simple cut allowing just a glimpse of her toes.

"My friend Jean is wicked good," Lisa added over Ava's shoulder as I took it all in and thought *wife of a diplomat*. No, the second wife, the one he left the mother of his kids for.

"Jesus fuckin' Christ," Sean said, and the compliments flowed from everyone in the room, the dog pushed out to see what the fuss was, and even the kids barreled into the kitchen to witness the celebrity in their midst. She stood lean and tall among them, a dark swan circled by barnyard chickens. Her eyes held mine but she said nothing, subtly rouged lips unsmiling.

I realized I was still holding a dripping forkful of cabbage and lowered it to my plate when Ava said, "Is it all right?"

"All right? Goddamn, we should take you out to Hollywood!" Sean shouted and Annabelle frowned, looking at five feet nine of trouble if she'd ever seen it.

I worked my mouth to find my voice and said, "It'll work for the job interview." A shadow of hurt passed over Ava's face and was gone.

"When do we go?" she asked.

- 3 -

I braced my hands on the guano-slimed gunwale to hide their tremor and concentrated on the distant lights of the city, the sounds of waves sloshing against the hull, the appealing stink of salt water full of life and corrupting corpses. My skin felt hot and gritty from too much time in the sun and the wind gently brushed my scalp.

Whiskey would steady my hands, but I needed my wits about me to deal with Grace, so I focused my thoughts on the uncounted corpses dumped into Boston Harbor, maybe below us right now, swaying like unholy kelp as they reached up with skinless fingers for the thrumming rumble of our engine.

"Phone buzzed, they're there." Sean called out from the pilothouse of the forty-foot fishing boat as we waited on the swells. Number Four would have pulled up to the club in a taxi borrowed from another cousin. Ava would go into the club alone.

I didn't like it but there wasn't any choice. Number Four looked like the Chelsea thug he was and Sean looked like he slept in his clothes. Me? They didn't let copier repairmen mingle with the Brahmin elite of Boston.

Ava wasn't interviewing with Grace to be a whore, exactly. The Brooks Brothers set would never be so crass. The best comparison was a genteel New England version of a Japanese hostess bar, where beautiful women fawned over wealthy men sipping scotch, laughing at their jokes and allowing them to remember their virility.

When the whoring came later, it wasn't at the club.

"Bunker Hill, where is it?" I called out and Sean walked up, easy on the shifting deck. "Bunker Hill, you know, where the big—"

"I know what fuckin' Bunker Hill is," Sean said and pointed in a direction that meant nothing to me. "Over there somewhere."

"Lot of people died."

"Yeah," Sean replied. "Redcoats marched right into our guns." *Our guns*, like he was there, but that was Boston. "And we had to hold fire until we could see the whites of their eyes. Cut 'em down like cordwood but they kept comin'."

"I wonder how many of the bodies they just bulldozed into the harbor."

"They didn't have bulldozers."

I shot him a look and he grinned, but his eyes were on the city lights, maybe hearing the echoes of a battle fought by his great-great-granddad.

"Hey, John. You in the Army?" He said *ah-me*. "That where you learned this stuff?"

I pictured my grandfather's old Army car with a sack of kittens tied to the tailpipe. "Never in the Army," I said. He was looking at me so I added, "I wanted to impress a girl."

He chewed on that for a minute before saying, "Bitches."

We both laughed and it was good to release the tension. I fished out a pack of cigarettes and pulled out two. He produced a lighter and did the honors, protecting the flame with one big hand.

"She's gonna do all right in there," he said once we were both lit.

"Who?"

"Your girl." Two simple words felt like a punch in the chest. "Ava's real sharp. Lisa won't stop talking about how cool she is."

Grace would spot Ava as soon as she hit the darkened interior. The lioness eyeing a new predator at the watering hole. She'd pull Ava aside to give her a warning or an invitation. Into her office. Ava would take out the little gun Sean loaned her, a Llama .32, and force Grace to open the discreet door that concealed a closet. The trapdoor in the floor of the closet would reveal a ladder down to the water. It was how the bigwigs came and went without making the newspapers.

I'd known about the back door for years, since I started working for Grace. Thinking one day I'd have to kill her.

Sean's phone buzzed a second time, which meant Ava had triggered her burner phone. He trotted back to the pilothouse without a word and a moment later the engine noise increased. I felt the bow rise as the stern dug in. The wind pressed against my face and shoved my hair back in subtle rejection of my choice, and we pushed through the waves toward the lights.

Unseen below, the forgotten dead wailed at our departure.

SEVENTEEN

- 1 -

Her name was Grace.

The place I took her was dark and wet and smelled of dead sea things. A circular room with a ceiling lost to darkness and old brick walls crusted with salt and slimed with mold. The staircase was more rust than iron where it spiraled up one wall, held to the bricks with wicked spikes. It was more than a hundred years old, the lighthouse, and empty for the last twenty. Built by immigrant laborers to guide trading craft into ports at Boston Town and fishermen south to safety.

I knelt before the small fire built of kindling brought from shore and laid the tools out on the hard floor, solid clanks that cut through the whoosh and bang of the waves outside. Wind pushed in through the door but I shielded the flames with my body, sunburned skin on my cheeks and forehead tingling from the new heat.

"What the fuck?" Sean said and I glanced at the shifting orange and black planes of his face. His eyes were big in the dark and I knew he had reached his limit.

"Go outside and keep an eye on the boat," I told him, and he left with shotgun to guard a rocky island maybe sixty feet across, featureless except for the tower.

I crossed over to the captive, her hands cuffed to the spiral stairs behind her and a clam sack over her head. I'd pissed on the sack before we took her and the stink of clams and urine had already caused her to vomit, a gleaming spill that dripped into the cleavage revealed by her torn evening gown. But she was a tough bitch, my Grace, and hadn't said a single word.

After standing close enough that she could feel my body heat for a good minute, I jerked the sack off hard enough to hurt and grabbed a fistful of her bleached hair, pulling her close enough that our noses touched.

"You speak and you die."

I stepped back then and she slumped, shivering but still not speaking, eyes focusing on me and what I represented.

Kneeling, I placed a finger across my lips before lifting up the metal wedge and hammer. "The currents are tricky and might wash you out, but they might wash you in to shore where you'll be found before the fish eat you. I'll remove your teeth with this wedge."

I placed those items down on the floor and lifted the hedge clipper, steel blades hooked like a raptor's beak. "I'll take off your fingers one by one with these before I remove your toes and scatter them over the side of the boat. Maybe I'll keep one on my keychain as a remembrance."

Her chest rose and fell but she still didn't speak, eyes focused, mind working the angles.

"All of this will happen while you're alive if you lie even once," I said. "Now…are you surprised to see me?"

She nodded and I said, "You can speak," and she said, "Yes."

"Who did you expect to see?"

"Bent nose guys from the North End, the old guys."

"Did you sell me out?"

She didn't hesitate. "Yes."

"To the mob?"

"Yes," she closed her eyes for a beat and then her gaze met mine. "And to those hillbilly mafia assholes in New Hampshire."

I sniffed in surprise. "Why weren't they waiting at the club?"

"They didn't think you'd come for me there so they set up at my condo."

"Didn't think?"

"Because I told them you'd take me at home. You work alone."

"I'm not that predictable."

"Yes, you are," she said. "You kill with your hands or with a knife. If you shoot you like to be close enough to hear the brains hit the wall."

I nodded because when someone is right, they're right. "Why did you think I'd take you? We've worked together for so long."

"You'd know it was me sold you out. You'd know it was me who knew where you were staying. Where you'd go. I'm the only person who would know that."

I didn't bother to ask why she'd betrayed me. I know what kind of choice the mob had offered her.

"Who's coming for me, Grace?"

She took a deep breath and the firelight didn't show her any kindness, picking out the wrinkles on her chest and the hollowness of her cheeks.

"Everyone is coming for you, Rooster, everyone. Tongs in New York were in touch before the mob grabbed me. But it was those New Hampshire dipshits who told me that the word was out, a hunting license, reward. There's even a goddamned website. Those Townie Mafia assholes are so cranked up on their own product they couldn't stop talking. Information on just about everyone you ever hit is on the site. All those people who lost someone are gunning for you."

"You know the thing? The URL?"

"No."

I walked a circle around the fire, smelling the smoke, listening to the waves. I heard the tock of the boat's hull against the crumbling pier outside.

"Well, that sucks," I said and she barked a gargoyle's laugh. "Why didn't you tell me?" I asked when I came back around to face her.

"I thought they'd kill you before you found out."

I nodded in respect because she didn't apologize once. Tough as nails, my Grace.

"Do you know who put out the hunting license?"

"No."

I watched her closely but didn't see a tick. Not that she would let one show.

"Do you want a chance to live?" I asked and that broke her, water welled up in her eyes as her lip trembled.

"Yes," she said, and there was a moment that it was going to work out, then Sean's shotgun let loose outside.

- 2 -

They came in smart, cutting their motor on the far side of the island and using oars to scoot around to where Sean sat in our boat.

Sean himself was nowhere to be found, and I knew that Old Man Atlantic had pulled him deep for an embrace.

I came out firing and fast, no rolling, no stunt bullshit. My first magazine was emptied in a matter of seconds and I reloaded as I charged them, half of them split between their own dark craft and the one I road in on.

The terrifying stutter of an automatic weapon chewed up the night as I scuttled across the bow of my boat and put two rounds into the nearest man while the second struggled to gain a clear shot. Bullets chewed up the railing as a long muzzle flash reached across the water like lighting from Hell but stopped when I closed on the other man, feeling the pluck of a bullet on my sleeve as he panicked and I didn't, and his brains splattered across the pilothouse.

His shotgun came to life in my hands, still warm from his grip, and I rushed behind my own thunder in a long leap to their boat, catching my foot and sprawling across the deck as the submachine gun emptied its magazine in a long burst. A futile attempt to kill the empty night.

The click and the curse were clear over the ringing in my ears and I knew he was empty.

I rose to one knee and blew out his pelvis while I charged through the sound of his howling, swinging my weapon wildly and feeling the crunch of his jaw as he toppled over the side and into the black sea. I was exultant in the knowledge that he would drown alone and in terror, and I think I was grinning.

The empty shotgun banged to the deck as I drew my Beretta and took aim at the back of the fourth man, but I was too slow to fire, and the quick-footed shit disappeared through the lighthouse door.

- 3 -

A different man would have gone through that door to save Grace, tough old Grace. But I am the Rooster, John Gallo to some and my business is killing.

I pressed my back against the bricks to the left of the door and tossed my jacket through where it was met by a spitting storm of automatic fire. There was a woman's scream from within, and I ducked inside to let loose a round as the submachine gun made its futile racket, another cheap thug who didn't understand his expensive toy and burned through ammunition in seconds.

The hollow bang of footsteps rang out and I knew that he was climbing the stairs. I waited until the sound circled around to the doorway and then stepped through, ripping off three quick shots to draw sparks from the stairs above me as he cursed and I saw motion across the way, even farther up.

She had worked her way loose, my darling Grace, and was racing up the stairs ahead of the hitman.

Inside deeper, running, firing, not giving him a chance to reload, and I registered the scream of metal too late as my nose filled with the odor of rust.

The stairs came tumbling down.

A flash of light filled my vision and then blackness. Only a moment of unconsciousness, I thought, because dust was still swirling and the clatter of tumbling bricks continued when reality swarmed back in.

My gun was no longer in my hand and my eager razor took its place. My left leg throbbed as I rose to follow the intermezzo of my target's whimpering. I traced my free hand over jags of twisted metal and saw the shine of his eyes before I made out his pinned form.

He offered his hand and I knelt on his wrist, showing him the sharp steel in his future. He cried like a child, and when I opened his belly he made barnyard sounds.

I paused as he gurgled and the shit leaked from him, listening for a sound from Grace who was not a friend but had been a partner of sorts for more than a decade. I saw no conflict between this feeling of loss and my earlier thoughts of dumping her mutilated body in the ocean.

Killer and sociopath, John Gallo and Rooster.

"Grace!" I shouted.

Grace offered no song of her own so I repositioned the razor and pushed it deep into his guts, wagging the blade from side to side to part his intestines. He bucked hard enough to shift the groaning iron atop him and I lost my metal fang in his rib cage.

No matter.

I dug my fingers into the slippery lengths of his stuffing and ripped her eulogy from his belly, standing to pull a handful of his best material forth into the air, saying only "Grace," as I worked her final honor.

He made the sounds I would wish on my enemies as their last while I hunted through the room, using my lighter left-handed as my right was so wet the device would not spark.

She was crushed and dead with half of her skull dented like a pothole in the street. The body came free with some effort and I carried her to the second boat, removing her head with a short axe I found clipped to the hull. Fire would destroy her fingerprints but not her teeth, but she would understand. Fist in her hair I tossed her head across the deep, hearing an ungracious plunk as it met water. My Grace was vain as an ingénue and would not want to be found so disfigured anyway.

The rest of her went to sea on a boat of fire, though to do so was foolish and would draw the police like crawling flies. But she was right when she said I had no one else. I raced quickly away in the boat I came in on and did not look back.

That was Grace.

- 4 -

I smelled death before I pushed open the door and entered the house with gun in hand, a courtesy weapon left on the boat by one of my victims.

What had once smelled of food and family and sounded with enough clamor to drive a man mad with laughter was as quiet as a tomb. I knew it was empty of life as I closed the door behind me and held my lighter up like a talisman.

I passed the front room on the way in and saw forms both crumpled and small. My fingers grew sticky when I felt their cold necks for a pulse and thought one of them was named Kevin.

A woman was on the stairs, her shirt ricked up to her ribs and her feet reaching the floor. At first I thought it was Lisa who had thought Ava was so cool, but realized this girl was built differently. Darker. Someone I didn't know. Was she a friend? A neighbor who chose the wrong time to visit?

Whoever she was, she had run, clever girl, but they shot her in the back before she could escape, and when she slid down to their lowly depth, they slapped her head open with a heavy caliber, something so big that not a strand of her bleached hair was visible. It offended me that she smelled of the various deadly stenches, and I briefly considered carrying her to a tub and filling it so that when she was found no one would know.

I did not do that thing.

In the heart of the house which strangers might call the kitchen, Annabelle lay on her belly, housedress yanked high enough to reveal her support hose. I knelt beside her and dropped the lighter to tug the dress down. Her body gave out an uncomfortable noise that I ignored because it was all I could do for her.

A sound made by a throat. Wheezy and whimpering. I cursed myself for not sensing his life already.

I crawled to the yellow dog and saw the gleam of his eyes, heard the magnificent thump of his tail striking the floor. I lifted the table quietly so as not to frighten the poor thing and told him he was smart to hide before realizing the great insult I had offered this yellow dog, he of the sloppy kisses and taste for ham. Looping trails of him led down the hall to the enormous rip in his stomach. Shotgun at close range. Every rise and fall of his ribs caused more to leak free.

"You went out and met the bastards, didn't you," I said and placed a hand on his skull as he wheezed. The room grew light enough to pick out details, and I knew then my eyes had filled with the blackness in my heart. I stroked his wet muzzle with one hand and said another eulogy as I placed the barrel of my new-found gun, a well-cared-for Glock, behind his ear.

"Good boy."

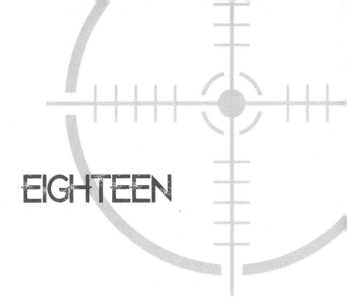

EIGHTEEN

Dawn was still a few hours away when I followed the sound of Aerosmith uphill toward Sully's bar, squatting like a sore in the scabrous neighborhood, oozing beer instead of puss. The glowing Schlitz sign was a lighthouse for the damned, drawing them in like moths to smash on the rocks of failure rather than warding them away.

Two bullets left in a borrowed 9mm. The straight razor was gone, left deep in a Mafioso's gut. The guy gifted me with a limp, so I called us even.

The bar's door banged open and two thickset men in Red Sox jerseys staggered out, crossing the street towards me. They raked me with belligerent glares as they floated past on a cloud of beer fumes.

I crossed the street through the splash of a cab's headlights and ignored the car horn. My left eye was sticky when I blinked and I wiped at the cut on my brow, smearing red on my forehead.

Voices climbed over the blare of a television but all of it was drowned in classic rock pounding from the juke. Ava was a pearl among swine, a diamond among steaming piles of shit. She had on a clinging tank top and jeans that ended halfway down her shins. Sneakers. The clothes were new and I remembered Sean's cousin Lisa bragging, "Jean's wicked good."

Ava drank at the bar like she owned the place, with Number Four by her side. She was nursing something in a martini glass while a small crowd of interested thugs hovered around trying to get her attention, tilting at windmills with green bottles in their fists instead of lances.

"Whiskey," I said and slapped a five-dollar bill into a puddle of beer on the bar. The bartender was a blue-haired punker ten years too old for a middy shirt, who snarled at my tone until her gaze met mine. Her eyes widened and her pupils narrowed as she considered options like fight or flight but settled on *stay quiet until the bad man passes.* She took the money like it was bait for a trap and poured me a shot, spilling more than a pro should.

I picked up the glass and swallowed foul-tasting liquid fire. Smacked the glass onto the wood and nodded. "Again."

She was pouring the second shot when the thugs took notice and Ava saw my reflection in the mirror.

I drank the next shot and put the glass down. Nodded at the bartender as my lungs began to smolder and smoke filled my mouth.

"Where's Sean?" Number Four was behind me now, spinning me around by the shoulder in excitement, not aggression, but I batted his hand away and turned back to my drink like I didn't know him.

He wasn't too bright, but one look at my face was all it took.

"Oh Jesus," he said, been around the block enough not to ask the pointless question.

"Who the fuck is this jokah?" a thug chirped in a surprisingly high-pitched voice accompanied by the whistle of air through a missing front tooth.

My eyes watered from the whiskey burn. I paused in the assault on my liver to touch fingers to my brow and study the pretty rubies I found on their tips.

"Italians," I said after a moment, chumming the water.

"The fuck you mean Italians?" the whistling thug said and Number Four grabbed the front of my shirt. "You tell ma? I gotta tell ma!"

"You can't go home," I growled, but he shoved me back. The wooden bar cracked my spine and pain flared through the whiskey fog. "Don't go home!"

"Fuck!" he bellowed and tried to turn away, but I hooked him hard in the neck with my right fist and he staggered. Tough as an ox he didn't go down, so I stomped the side of his knee and he hit the floorboards with a shout, clutching the wounded joint.

"You're dead!" Whistler roared and looped a wild right. I threw my left arm up tight to my ear and caught the blow even as I stepped inside his reach and snapped my elbow down across his nose. He sat down hard and the heel of my shoe connected with his forehead.

"Stop!" Ava grabbing my arm then, pulling me through the growing mass of men. "Let's go!" She pushed through the door and down the single step where I jerked free and turned back, discovering the pistol in my fist.

"Give it to me," Ava hissed.

The bloody face of the whistler appeared in the doorway but he skidded to a halt at the sight of the gun.

"Give it to me!"

I relaxed my grip and let Ava peel the pistol from my hand. She backed away and aimed the weapon at my face. I tried to say something.

"Wait—"

She shot me.

NINETEEN

- 1 -

Dead.

- 2 -

It was good to be dead. Dead meant rest. Dead meant no one trying to kill me.

Meant not thinking about Ava. About being played for a fool.

"What?"

Was I dead?

"No, but you're fuckin' heavy."

"Was I talking out loud?

"Yeah." A man's voice, thick with south Boston. "Give him another fuckin' pill, all right?"

My head was a balloon barely tethered to my neck. Vast and swollen. Vision swam into being, narrow and dark. Something was wrong with it. Speckled. A face hovered over mine and I saw crooked teeth behind gleaming lips, the pink tip of a tongue protruding between them. Something about the small chin told me it was a woman.

"My face is huge," I slurred.

"Christ," the man's voice said. "She shot him retarded."

"Shut up." The woman. "That's the pills."

"Pills?" That was my voice, sloppy as a three-day drunk.

"My friend's a vet, he hooks me up."

Pieces of broken memory were sliding back together to form a whole, but the bright muzzle flash didn't bother me much.

That vet had some great shit.

"She was too good for you," the woman said. I thought her name might be Lisa and said as much.

"Yeah." Lisa held up a shining needle and worked thread through the end. "I knew she was too good for us, swannin' around ma's house with that way she talked. That fuckin' cabbage on the stove, stinks like farts." She worked a tiny knot into the thread and tightened it with her teeth. "But how stupid can you be? How didn't you see she was too good for you?"

The point of the needle descended and I felt the tug of thread through my skin before my neck finally came unglued and my head floated toward the white ceiling.

- 3 -

They moved me to a small room without lights where I slept. I woke once when a burly man jammed an IV needle into my arm. A medical degree by mail type, he only needed four tries to find the vein.

I coughed. There was a bad smell. Me.

"He's awake," the gap-toothed man called out to someone unseen, his voice whistling and high pitched. It wasn't until he left that I recognized him as the whistler from Sully's Bar.

The second time I awakened as cold water sluiced across my body. I was sprawled naked on the wooden floor while Lisa emptied a plastic bucket of soapy water down the length of my body, moving in an out of the light streaming through the doorway.

My face was throbbing and when I tried to touch it, my arm rose with all the grace of a crane at Boston Sand & Gravel. A spiderweb of fire spread across my skull when my hand made contact with the mountain of bandages burying the left side of my face.

She was too good for you.

A bright muzzle flash.

Ava got them all killed. Grace. Sean. Annabelle. Almost killed me.

"Do you know where you are?" Lisa asked, bucket dangling from one hand.

"No." My voice was a dry croak.

Who the hell was Ava?

How did she put this all together?

Why did she want me dead?

"Do you know what happened?"

"Shot." That wasn't the half of it. Ava had played me like a fool. Summoned up my past to take me off the count.

Lisa crouched with the easy strength of a young woman and picked up a towel from the floor, wiping down my chest. "It's been two days and we gotta move you. Can you help?"

"Yes."

I lifted my ten-ton head and tried to brace my elbows beneath me. The room spun and I slumped, fighting a surge of nausea.

"Shit." Lisa tossed aside the towel. I guess she wasn't paid enough to dry off strange dick.

"Let me try again." The words dribbled out of my mouth without conviction, but I rolled to my right side and pulled my knees toward my chest. A minute later I was on my hands and knees. "Help me."

She was strong and did most of the work but eventually I was on my feet.

"Let's go."

"You need pants." She shook her head, hair bunched on top in a flopping ponytail. "I gotta put a smaller bandage on your face. You look like the Elephant Man."

- 4 -

We were outbound on the MBTA Orange line. Lisa's doing. I don't remember much. I wore a dark sweatshirt with the hood pulled up, hiding the bandages on my cheek unless someone looked right at me. My left eye blinked continuously, leaking tears. I suspected powder burns on my eye and vision on that side was blurry, with black grains like cracked pepper scattered across my view. I wondered if it would recover.

"Took a piece out of your cheekbone back near the sideburn," Lisa said. "Gonna have a dent in your skull even after it heals."

The doors whooshed open and we slipped off the train in the shithole of Malden where we found a waiting Nissan with doors in shades of primer and an interior done in Burger King wrappers.

Lisa nodded at the glovebox and I pulled out a crumpled paper bag with my pistol inside it. The magazine was empty but there was a single round chambered.

My last bullet.

"Bitch dropped it after she shot you." She keyed the ignition and backed out of the space. "Want to tell me what happened?"

It wasn't until we were driving northbound on Route 3 that I told her. "Her name was Grace."

TWENTY

Lisa stayed in the car as I walked across the sandy asphalt of the rest stop parking lot until I found a picnic table far from the stink of the toilets. There were a few other vehicles parked nearby, and one young guy with a ponytail was walking his beagle along the grassy verge. Cars hissed by on the highway just past the stand of trees, and a brown hawk circled lazily overhead, hunting roadkill.

The pain was back, a steel vice on the side of my face, but I didn't want the pills yet.

There was a seat in the sun and I made it mine, feeling warmth on my head and shoulders. Sweat beaded along my hairline beneath the hood but I ignored it.

All of them dead.

I had almost relocated to Boston several times over the years, but I could never escape the feeling of hopelessness that overcame me each time I was in town. There were so many things about the place that I liked…

Sean's family dead.

…the seafood, different from New York's. I could eat two pounds of fried clams at a sitting and I'd even learned to enjoy steamers, though that took some convincing…

The yellow dog torn up, ribs heaving.

…I'd been to Fenway Park more than once and enjoyed the instant camaraderie of the place, though as a New Yorker I could never admit it…

The house smelled like blood and shit.

…but if I told you about Boston, my Boston, it wouldn't be any of those things, nor of the jobs I'd worked. My Boston was a wide set of stone steps that led straight down into the green harbor to depths unimaginable and menacing. If I stood on the steps and lifted my gaze the frosted waves stretched out into eternity and I unraveled.

It was the edge of the world beckoning me forward to take one more step down into the water, another and another until the water closed over my head.

I would never be returning to Boston, this I knew, but I was taking the feelings inspired by the stone steps with me. They reminded me of the city's message for me on every visit.

This will end badly.

This will end in sorrow.

I felt a hot prickling behind my eyes and touched my face, surprised to find wetness. No, not surprised, not really. My black dog was sinking fangs into my forehead, eating my brain. It would kill me this time. I needed medication. More of Lisa's pills. I needed a cave in which to hole up with enough booze to put me the fuck out. To render me immobile.

They were coming. All of them. Every organized crime outfit I'd ever hit. The Italians had tough men with guns, the Armenians lived a life of vendetta and the Russians were bug-shit crazy when it came to violence.

Chin would come. He would find me.

They would kill me. Make it a display.

Would Ava cheer when I died? It didn't matter. She'd be found in a dumpster long after the rats had their way with her.

I waited long enough that Lisa finally braved the public restroom, and when she was inside I stuck a stack of bills beneath the windshield of her Nissan, the black dog padding by my side. They fluttered and beckoned and would give her my message.

Behind the restroom building I discovered a trail leading into the trees, and beyond the woods I could see the glitter of sun on windows. Nashua, I thought.

The dog led me down.

TWENTY-ONE

- 1 -

"You drunk?"

The needle whirred and I felt the sting but ignored it, concentrating as I was on slipping the flask one-handed from my back pocket. I opened it with my teeth, the metal taste staining my tongue, and took a sip.

"No," I said through a sour mash sigh.

Pink Floyd was shimmering from the speakers and I blinked, looking around as if to see David Gilmour crouching amidst the file cabinets and reclining chairs in the tattoo parlor. Thin ribbons of smoke rose from two incense sticks jammed into a pot alongside a dead plant—smoking kills—and I had an idea.

"Know where I can score some weed?" I asked.

"No," he said.

"Coke?"

"No."

He was a fat kid with black eyeliner, a black T-shirt and black Dickies over black Frye boots. I had a terrible thought and jerked in the chair, feeling a jab in my arm.

"Don't move," he said, glaring at me through those raccoon eyes and flipping his bangs back with a jerk of his head.

"I have a question."

"What?"

"Are you color blind?"

"What?"

"Are you color blind? Is that why you said go with black ink instead of color?"

He puffed his cheeks in disgust. Not a good look for a fat kid. "We couldn't use color because yellow won't show up on your skin. Remember?"

I nodded, noticing now with his chin lifted that the paperclips pierced through the skin of his neck were affixed with a clear adhesive band. I fought down a snicker that might have turned into a belly laugh.

I was seriously fucking drunk.

"I'm sorry, please keep going," I said and leaned back, eyes tracking up the faded rock posters on the wall to see the made-up monsters of Kiss staring down at me from the ceiling. I shook off their glare and glanced around the small place, fake wood paneling on the wall, stained ceiling, two more chairs. There were no windows in the back room where we were joined in our creative dance, but I could see grey light leaking in through the dirty window in the foyer. The smell of sweat lurked beneath the incense.

Sip.

We were the only two in the place and there was a bell over the door to tell me if we had company.

Sip.

A DJ came on over the speakers shouting, "Sunday, Sunday, Sunday!" and I was so irritated that I almost shot the radio before I remembered to conserve ammo. One bullet left.

Another hit off the flask helped me through the next song without being too much of an asshole, but when I offered him a sip and he said, "No," I blurted out, "Vegan." He squinted at me like he was going to tell me to fuck off but just shook his head and puffed his cheeks again.

Even through my amber haze the gun was eating into the base of my spine. I thought about laying it on the table, but the little phony would probably call the cops.

"All right," he said, leaning back with a grunt of effort. Jesus, kid probably hadn't done a single push up in his life.

"All right what?"

"All right done," he said, and I sat up with my own grunt, feeling a dull throb of pain in my healing ribs as I studied the cunningly depicted paw, black ink sharp against the skin inside my forearm. Even with the redness and mild swelling, it looked brilliant.

I squinted and leaned down to study the chicken scratch below the paw.

"You fuckin' sign your name? What's that?"

He jerked as if he'd been slapped, and I wondered what he saw sitting in his chair.

"It's Chinese," he said, voice tight. "Yellow Dog. I couldn't give you the color but I could do the words. The characters looked cooler than English would've."

I looked at the Chinese and pictured the dog beneath the table. My vision blurred and I fought the tide of emotions pressing against my control. A bull leaning against a kitchen door. Thin wood that wouldn't hold long.

"This is good," I said, swinging my feet to the floor and standing up. I lifted my arm in front of me and looked at the paw. Clenched my fist and watched the knotted muscles in my forearm writhe. "You do good work, kid."

He looked relieved and somehow pleased. Kid like him is not used to praise.

"Was that your dog?" he asked.

"Yeah." I owned his death, at least.

I pulled out my wad of cash and peeled off twice what he'd quoted as a price. I noticed that he was wearing cake makeup and that beneath the spread-on illusion were the bumps of pimples.

In the cramped foyer I was struck with the smell of disinfectant fighting for control against the incense and my stomach lurched. I needed air.

My hand was on the doorknob when his voice slipped over my shoulder and sang me a ballad.

"I can get you hash."

She was good looking and honey-blonde with a bit too much nose, working the whiskey bottle like a pro, no flash but no splash, and she gave me a healthy pour.

She rapped her knuckles on the bar to let me know it was on her, and I put down a couple singles. Be quiet and tip well and the bartender is your friend.

It was a dark place and needed a good cleaning, maybe with a fire hose. A chipped wooden bar wrapped around a central island of bottles that flashed with muted colors in the dusty light, as if the light spectrum itself was tired and only here because there was no place else to go. I'd never been in the place before, but I'd spent a lot of my life on the same stool. The Holiday is everywhere if you know where to look, or to bleed the right kind of hopelessness.

I heard the crack of billiards and a curse. Turned on my stool to take in the two young guys playing pool, baseball caps on backwards. One dangled a ciggy from the corner of his mouth. A heavyset woman at the end of the bar was alternately playing a video keno game and reading a beat-up paperback by Danielle Steele. At the other side of the bar was a hollow-cheeked guy in a filthy work shirt, maybe green, maybe blue. He had a pitcher going and a lit cigarette in an ashtray beside him, his eyes spending too much time on me. Sullen, beady things glinting deep inside sockets like caves. Mine shafts. I wondered how much space he had inside his oddly shaped skull for a brain and why he was pickling what there was.

He barely moved from his stool, a bar-mounted gargoyle built from the twin cancers: despair and alcohol. At one point he shuffled past, and I heard the clink of coins before the thump of a pack of cigarettes from a brown machine with its myriad brands advertised in faded colors.

He moved by again leaving a rank, unwashed smell in his wake. An old man smell. He was a cliché and bought Camels. Used bar matches to light up, the butt held in the V of yellowed fingers as narrow as the cigarette. He dragged deep, stifling a cough.

"Fuck," I said, not nearly wasted enough. I banged back the liquor and coughed as a few drops tried to annex my lungs.

"Going pretty hard pretty early, huh?" the bartender said with an accent thick enough to stop a bullet.

"That's just it," I said and waved at the rays of murky light leaking through slats in the venetian blinds. "Still light. Soon as that's gone, I have to head home."

"Night job?"

"Sleep. Big day tomorrow."

I uncurled my fingers and the glass moseyed across the rough wood at the prodding of my fingernails. She refilled it with extra for luck and I smiled.

"What's your name?" she asked through an answering grin that showed crooked teeth. I could tell by the way she ignored the bandage on my face that she'd been around and seen it all.

"John Gallo," I said because that was the license I was carrying. My right hand was filled with the glass so I awkwardly offered my left hand. She had a working girl's grip, no fooling around.

"Ambuh."

Ambuh? Took my whiskey-soaked translator a second to spit back *Amber*.

"Meetcha," she said and turned my hand over to see the colors exposed when my cuff slipped back. She gave me a quick glance for permission and pushed my cuff up a few more inches until she could make out enough of the work to know what it was. "Looks good, but old. Why a rooster?"

I tapped my chest with my free hand, not minding the touch of her fingers on my wrist. "Gallo," I said before switching to the Spanish pronunciation. "*Gallo*."

The fingers of my captive hand stretched and took her wrist, gently reversing the control and turning her arm to make out the wavering length of a tail with a pointed tip inked along the inside of her arm. I raised an eyebrow and she gave me something that was half laugh and half sigh.

"I was in a band out in LA," she said, eyes drifting up and to the right. I couldn't tell from her expression whether she saw something she missed or regretted. "An all-girl group called Tail. We played the Roxy once."

"On Sunset."

"Yeah."

I released her hand and sipped my whiskey while she braced her elbows on the bar. Curses and laughter from the pool table and the clicking sound of racking balls for a new game. A car horn honked outside.

"One night the lead guitarist fell off the stage. The reviewer called it the *fall of the New York Dolls*." She took a beat, and I nodded to let her know I got the gist. The Dolls were a punk group with men dressed as women. It wasn't meant as a compliment. "We were at an after-party somewhere in Hollywood, you know, one of those nights bouncing from place to place, and the singer starts screaming about… shit, I don't even remember. Anyway, she had on this shirt that read: WHO NEEDS BRAINS WHEN WE HAVE BEER. And I thought, this isn't my life and left."

"To work in a bar," I said.

"Yup."

"In Nashua."

"Beats Brockton."

I wasn't sure what that meant, but she was pouring one out for both of us so I kept my lip zipped.

"Anyway, I played bass." She lifted her glass and we clinked over the bar, both of us knocking the stuff back like it was water before she turned away to grab a remote control. She aimed it at a hunched shape in the corner near the pool table. Red digits sprang to life with an ominous flicker. "I just put ten credits on the juke. How 'bout you pick some tunes? But no fucking Styx."

Light and sound flooded the bar when the door opened, and I could taste the oily grit from nearby roadwork on my tongue. My friend from the tattoo parlor clomped inside with two more vampires of the taller and thinner variety. The twins took a seat at the bar near the keno lady and Captain Inky met my eyes before jerking his head toward the men's room.

Amber eyed the newcomers like she knew who they were. I caught her disappointed look when I pushed back off my stool. She turned away without a word, and I couldn't tell you why it hurt a bit.

On the way back I caught a muttered, "Faggot," from the man in the dirty work shirt. If I'd been able to muster enough anger to take a swing, I might have had a chance of seeing the dawn. But I was floating toward the drain on a river of amber liquor and didn't give a shit.

In the cramped bathroom I took care of business and left with an empty bladder and lighter wallet. Kind soul that he was, Captain Inky threw in a small copper pipe. "Don't say I never gave you anything," he said. Something he heard somewhere and tried to pass off as his own.

Amber was busy washing beer glasses when I left.

- 3 -

I walked out into a world bleached of color by a bullying sun. A world of black and white houses crowding the narrow street, paint chipped, never to be retouched. Fans in the windows because welfare didn't pay for air conditioning. I saw a series of round white blurs looking out, details of their faces dissolving. The lucky ones resting before another third shift in hell. Eating starch and crap, television telling them how their lives could be, *should* be, while their arteries hardened. I stumbled over a rusting bicycle without tires. It was chained to a street sign next to a broken Big Wheel, the plastic faded by the sun.

I coughed against the grit and toxic stink enveloping the crew grading the street. Watched as lean brown and white men with rags over their faces dragged and scraped hot asphalt with rakes, their orange vests hanging limp, hardhats transforming the crowns of their heads to saunas.

At the corner a stop sign. I turned right. Weeds grew up from the sidewalk, and an old Chevy station wagon full of kids wheezed past. Somewhere a radio crackled with a baseball game. A sob broke from my throat with all the elegance of a meaty belch. I missed my city, my sidewalks, the oily humidity of a subway platform and the buzz of languages telling me every day, *the horizon is that way!*

Subways, cars, taxis, bicycles weaving in and out.

I pulled open a screen door and stepped into the steamy heat of the Nashua Panthers House of Pizza. Behind the counter a middle-aged Hispanic man eyed my bandages while I slurred my order.

"Meatball sub."

"Large or small?"

"I dunno. Large."

I put a twenty on the counter and walked out of the shop to get some air, bracing a hand on the wall of the alley beside the shop. My head swam and my stomach fired the first shots of rebellion.

My concentration was directed toward puking up a stream of yellow gunk and I nearly fell face forward into the mess when I heard the voice behind me.

"Hermano?"

I stumbled, foot skidding through the puddle and whirled around, but it was only the counterman, all five feet nothing of him. He wore the expression of a man who has seen it all, but his eyes crinkled with something I couldn't identify.

"Estas bien?" he asked.

"Si."

He braced his hands on his hips. *"Por que estas llorando?"*

"I'm not crying," I said and wiped at my eyes to prove it. *"No estoy llorando."*

"Entrar, en la cocina," he said, gesturing to a door. I could hear busy kitchen sounds inside. *"Todo estara bien."* It will be all right.

He reminded me a little of the people at The Quiet Man, solid, aware and generous. Though if he was Irish, it was by way of Guadalajara.

"De donde eres…" I attempted as whiskey swarmed over the banks and flooded the part of my brain that knew Spanish. Somehow he understood and said, "Ensenada."

I pulled out my cigarettes but needed his help to bring the flame to the jittering tip of the Viceroy stabbed between my lips. *"Gracias,"* I said through a cloud of smoke.

"Beto?" I heard a voice from the doorway and saw a squat woman watching me. The smell of vomit abruptly levitated up off the alley floor to create an unholy alliance with the stink of pizza sauce.

I felt my stomach clench. I pushed past the counterman and he let himself be moved, though he had about as much give to him as a fire hydrant.

"*Hermano, aqui.*" Brother, here.

The words deflected off my back like spent musket balls and I picked up my pace.

"*Hermano!*"

I turned another corner and dragged the back of my wrist across my eyes, stumbling onto Main Street where the traffic rumbled by, and the stores carried clothing priced out of reach of the people who lived in apartments just a few blocks off the main drag.

Claws clicked on the sidewalk and I detected the panting of my black-furred friend as he trotted by my side. I reached elegant tables outside of a restaurant where well-dressed people sipped Pinot Grigio and lounged in wicker chairs. I asked for a seat among them, outside where my dog would be allowed. The umbrellas would give us shade.

"What dog?" the kid in the white shirt and black trousers asked with a wary look.

"My black dog," I said, slurring despite my effort at clarity. "Black dog, yellow dog. I've heard of a red-nosed pit bull and a blue-dog republican."

"What?" he said, hands tightening on the menu he held before his chest like a shield. I wondered if I'd been speaking aloud. "Are you high?" he asked and I laughed.

A woman—hell, girl, she couldn't have had more than two years on the kid—came up to his left, smiled and gently hipped him aside as she looked at a book on the host stand.

"We're only seating reservations now, sir," she said, and I could tell from her diction that she had worked hard to cut back the tree-covered hills in her accent. "I can seat you at nine thirty tonight if you like?"

I waved off the idea of being awake at such an ungodly hour and thought about saying, "No thank you," but the effort was too much. I looked up the sidewalk as my dog cantered away.

An alcohol-soaked mechanism in my brain suggested that either she or my brother the pizza maker might call the police, not out of spite but out of concern. Embracing a vague sense of purpose, I moved in the direction of the low motel building a few blocks away where I knew my dog would be waiting.

My pockets were heavy with a hash pipe and a pistol with one round as I said goodbye to the afternoon.

- 4 -

It was cramped and dark, the ceiling stained and the carpet some kind of artificial turf. Green. Easy to clean with a garden hose was my guess. Might explain why the room was so damp and stank of mildew. Even the sheets on the bed were clammy.

A war movie raged on TV as I sat at the crooked table and dropped the small bit of black hashish onto the screen nestled in the bowl. The pipe met my lips and I sucked the flame of my lighter down into the hash, inhaling rough smoke that set off a series of coughs like aftershocks from an earthquake.

Through the thin wall behind the bed, I heard two men fighting. It made me want to weep, a couple in pain. Then they laughed and I realized with a smile they were as booze shot as I was.

The light was fading outside when I closed the blinds and peeled off my clothes, moving with a swimming motion as if deep under water while I dropped my shirt, pants and underwear to form an archipelago of fabric.

In the cramped bathroom I tugged the bandages from the side of my face and dropped them on the floor, studying the bruised sunrise covering my cheek, shades of purple and red with a stitched gash running through the middle like an ugly equator. Black threads protruded from my skin like the legs of an insect, and I imagined that a millimeter to the right and Ava's bullet would have blasted inward to ricochet inside my skull instead of deflecting off into the night.

Sweat beaded on my skin as I sat again and stripped down the Glock. I was self-taught, an autodidact of murder. I remembered my first Glock. Weird fucking gun designed by an Austrian watchmaker. I had to watch a video online to strip it down that first time. The first video I found had a young beauty in vintage lingerie who patiently explained the process while demonstrating. The lady knew her shit, but I still doubted she was hired for her skill.

With numb fingers I separated the weapon into thirty-five separate parts on the table before me, only dropping the recoil spring assembly. I wiped it off carefully to remove any lint before I prepared another pipe and puffed messianic clouds of poison into the air, rendering the atmosphere of the room as toxic as my mind.

When the weapon was reassembled, I wrote with simple directness on the hotel stationary and picked up the shiny brass shape of the 9mm bullet, racking the slide and feeding it into the pipe. When the slide closed with a purposeful snick, the round was loaded and the weapon was primed. This was no revolver. There would be no roulette.

I placed the weapon on the nightstand and stretched out naked atop the scratchy sheets as the war continued on television.

- 5 -

I woke up in the dark, fumbling at the sharp pain on my belly. A hoarse sound trying to pass for a laugh clawed up from my throat when I felt the sticky square of hotel stationary thumbtacked to my skin. I left it there to add color for whoever came to investigate the stink.

I can be a funny drunk.

My gorge rose and I coughed to fight it back, eyes unfocused, unable to process the dim surround. I was going to be sick and decided, quite rationally, why wait for that?

My left hand, the dumb one no matter how much I trained with it, fumbled at the nightstand and knocked the phone to the floor before discovering the squared-off form of the Glock. Ugly even by feel.

I jammed the business end of the barrel in my left ear and pulled the trigger.

The click was underwhelming.

"The fuck?" I slurred, somewhere between hungover and drunk. I passed the weapon over my chest to my smart hand and stuck the charcoal tasting barrel in my mouth.

Click.

"Gimme a break." My teeth banged on the barrel and it hurt, but not too much.

I could barely make out the pistol in the dark but I worked the slide over my chest, expecting to feel the tap of the bullet falling on my sternum.

No joy.

I sat up and the world spun while magma rose from deep within me. That made me laugh, hollow man that I was, and I stumbled to the blinds to shed light on my screwed-up suicide. Not even my night dog was with me now. He was back inside me where he belonged, barking and slavering with urgency.

The cord fought me so I ripped it down and the blinds rattled up, the faint glow of false dawn asking permission to come inside like a weak and dying vampire.

A bullet in the caliber of 9mm stood on the window sill.

I heard the creak of leather and turned, room revolving slowly to catch up with my movement. A silhouette leaned against the bathroom doorway.

"You shit."

"Ava?"

"Even now?"

The voice recognizable but not Ava's. The hair was too light in color, the shoulders too broad. Metal chains jingled, and the bathroom light behind her sparked to life. I saw the white of her eyes and the small jaw, not weak but refined despite her working-class background. She wore a leather jacket with metal chains and the blonde hair was down, bouncing off her shoulders. She looked like a torch on fire.

Lisa.

I heard the clomp of her heavy boots, made out stained jeans and saw she had on a black tank top beneath the jacket. Something metal dangled from her left ear and her nose was pierced.

Her lips were pressed tightly together and the wad of bills appeared, expanding from her hand like a stage magician producing flowers. They blew around me, into me, a cloud of fluttering green.

"You still wasted?" she asked.

"Little bit."

She plucked the bloody note from my chest and dropped it on the floor. Sluggish machines sputtered in my brain, iron gears grating against the inside of my skull. "You do that?"

She punched me in the ribs. Not some girlish punch, she stepped in and hooked me hard, and when her knuckles met my side a mushroom cloud of expanding fire burned through my torso.

I lost a few seconds and came back to discover myself propped on my elbows as her right boot lashed out to render me *castrato*.

Doc Marten's. Nice.

I twisted out of reflex, rolling on my side and getting my shin in front of the boot. The impact was painful but not crippling and she fell back, knocking over the chair in an attempt to catch herself.

She was up before I got off my knees and an object flew from her hand to batter my mouth. I felt my lip split through the chemical fog and the thing hit the ground, a smallish box splitting open. Brass tumbled across the green carpet.

Bullets.

They were 9mm rounds scattered like popcorn at a movie theater. The box read: FIOCCHI EXTREMA 9MM AMMO 115 GRAIN XTP JHP.

"Those are the best bullets they make for your gun," Lisa said, righting the table. "I asked the guy at the store."

I knelt to scoop loose rounds into the box. I knew there would be fifty in total. Her boot nearly stepped on my fingers, and I pulled my hand back.

"These are work bullets for a man with a job," she said. "Not your pussy suicide shit."

She took the bullet off the window sill and pulled down the front of her tank top, sliding the shiny death dealer into the black lace of her bra. "You get this one back when you're done."

"Done with what?"

"You have a job."

"What?"

"You have a client."

"What?"

She pursed her lips and I saw they were outlined in black. The metal dangling from her ear was a silver skull, and she creaked, clanked and clomped when she moved around the small room. She looked like she'd kill you after she fucked you, and even knowing that, you'd take her to bed.

I realized this was the first time I was seeing the real Lisa. Not Sean's cousin. Not the townie that was so impressed with Ava.

"You stink," she said. "Take a shower and sober up. I have to get some things."

I opened my mouth and she held out a hand. "You say 'what' again and I will save you the effort of committing suicide."

She banged over to the door, ass rolling in her jeans, and even through the haze I felt myself harden. The door slammed behind her while I knelt amidst the bullets and bucks and I finally closed my mouth.

"Holy shit."

I rose, holding my ribs, and limped into the bathroom, tiles grimy beneath my feet. My eyes were dark pits in a starving face, the overhead lamp painting diagonal slashes of sallow light across my face. A one-man terminal ward.

Ava's death kiss marked the side of my face like a missed promise.

I laughed, a guttural sound. Compressed my lips as I braced my hands on the sink and panted, internal compass swinging wildly as it struggled to find the true north of my death. Something of equal power fought this thing and dragged at the needle with brute strength. Sweat beaded on my forehead and I considered the bullets scattered on the floor. The pistol she left in the room.

Not for my pussy suicide shit. Punching the mirror seemed needlessly dramatic, but I did it anyway out of spite, weakness and hate. The blood welling from my knuckles flooded across dry gulches of calluses and scarring. My hollow cheeks sucked into something pathetic and ugly as poisoned water leaked from the corner of my eyes.

Not for pussy suicide shit.

I climbed carefully into the shower before the gleam of live ammo could lure me with its siren song, the flat clap of a weapon fired in a shitty hotel room. I turned the water on as hot as I could stand so I could sweat the shit out of my body, but I grew dizzy and wilted beneath the heat, sinking to my knees.

Beneath the roar of the spray and the drumbeat against the shower curtain, I detected the absence of my howling companion, my fanged guarantor of release.

But the goddamned yellow dog was with me when the cowardly black hound fled. The one who went out and met the gunman and died for my sins. He crouched, snarling on my arm.

Of their own accord my hands flew out to catch me before my body bucked and arched in transformation.

The needle swung.

Bile splattered between my hands, the sound horrible and pain tremendous.

A streak of brown swirled down the drain.

TWENTY-TWO

- 1 -

"Move again and I'll cut your throat."

I went still as the cold steel of a straight razor rested against my carotid artery.

"The bleach on my hair is burning," I said.

"Poor baby," Lisa said and dragged the blade up toward my jaw.

I sat on the floor with a towel around my hips as she shaved me, her legs against my shoulders on either side as she perched above and behind me on the bed.

"Stop trying to see."

I sighed and enjoyed the smell of her, the sweat from her body, the nicotine on her fingers. If I leaned a little to the left, I could catch her reflection in the mirror near the bathroom door. She'd taken off the tank top to "avoid getting this white shit on it" and holding the straight razor presented an image straight out of a fetish video. The kind on a pay site, none of that free shit.

I felt and heard the scrape of the blade along my jugular as the burning itch returned in force, ants covering my scalp, burrowing into the bone beneath.

"Better not be red," I muttered without moving my jaw much.

"It's blond," she whispered, breath hot on my ear. "Like almost white. Like that killer guy in the movie, the pretend human Harrison

Ford had to waste."

"Roy Batty," I said. I live a solitary life and know my movies. *"Blade Runner."*

Another caress of her breath tickled my ear. "Shut up."

She'd already cut my hair into a buzzed mess. "Not a goatee," I said when she produced the straight razor and shaving cream.

"Yes, a goatee," she'd said. "And a soul patch. Side burns. No mustache."

"Fuck me."

"You wish."

I closed my eyes and let the grooming relax me. Headache easing from the ibuprofen. Stomach easing from some red syrup in a bottle. Cherry flavor my ass.

"Why were you gonna do it?" Her voice was thick with emotion. One small syllable loaded with a case of TNT.

I stiffened and felt a thin line of heat on my neck as the steel bit me. She froze.

"Not now," I said quietly, and I felt her breasts shift against my back as she nodded.

"Okay," she said. "Will you try again?"

I lifted my right forearm and saw the new ink. Clenched my fist and made the paw jump.

"What's that?" she asked.

"Yellow dog."

After a solid minute of us just breathing she resumed her work and then wiped my neck and face with a towel. Smears of red tinged the white cream on the terry cloth.

"Get up," she said, standing and half trying to lift me which turned something simple into something clumsy. We managed, and she led me by the hand to the bathtub.

"On your knees," she said and I knelt, the tiles not comfortable, but she was pushing me forward with fingertips against my spine and rinsed the chemicals from my hair beneath the flowing water.

The relief was palpable as the bleach was washed away.

She eased me back and toweled me off, and I was disappointed when it stopped. Surprised to hear her boots clomping away.

"Hey," I said, turning on my knees in time to see her reaching her hands up and back behind her. The bra fell to the floor.

I followed her to bed.

- 2 -

I roused myself from a drifting fog when the mattress shifted and Lisa rose from bed. It was a sight worth seeing, so I propped myself up on my elbow for a better view.

"Hey," I said when she hooked a toe beneath her underwear and flicked it up off the floor to catch it. The jeans took flight next.

She looked at me. "Put on some pants."

"What?"

She slithered into the tank top without a bra.

"You'll get arrested if you go out like that," I said. "Or cause an accident."

Her smile was tighter than it should be when the door shook under a heavy fist. I sat up quickly and looked for the Glock.

"Who's that?" I asked.

"Your client appointment." She tossed a new but beat-up pair of jeans to me and I stood, slipping them on as she unlocked the door and opened it a crack. I heard the murmur of voices before she stepped back.

Number Four limped into the room.

My heart stuttered in my chest and I felt the sweat break out on my forehead. He looked terrible and drawn despite his bulk. His eyes were bloodshot, and I had a moment to wonder what he was on before I realized he'd been crying.

He met my eyes and I wouldn't do him the dishonor of looking away. His gaze dropped first and Lisa wrapped him in an embrace. She kissed his cheek before releasing him and slinging on her leather jacket.

"I'm going out for smokes."

Then she was gone, door left open behind her. Number Four looked at me nervously, belly straining against his green Celtics tank top, a Red Sox cap reversed on his head.

"Can I come in?"

"Of course," I said and waved to the cheap table and the tilted chair. I picked up the black T-shirt Lisa had bought for me, SLAYER writ jaggedly across the chest.

I sat on the bed, embarrassed that I had nothing to offer him until I spied an inch of whiskey left in a bottle leaning against the wall.

"Want a knock?" Off his nod I grabbed the whiskey and handed it to him with much creaking of bedsprings, not leaving the bed to make the transfer. He tilted the bottle back and sucked down the hooch. Coughed and rubbed his eyes.

We sat there silently as he looked at his feet and I looked at him and finally picked up the crumpled pack of Viceroys from the night-stand. I lit two, the smoke making me queasy, and handed one to him.

"Thanks," he said.

After a minute of us clouding the room with smoke I began, "What can—"

An invisible fist yanked his head up by the hair and hot eyes leak-ing pain grabbed my gaze, holding it in a vice grip. "Kill them," he said. "I want you to kill them."

I knew who he meant but I said, "Who?"

"The motherfuckers who did that to my family."

I waited.

"Sean told me you were worried about Mafia. Russians. And Japa-nese. And Chinese, all them," he hissed and spittle coated his bottom lip with white pearls. "Some redneck assholes up here in New Hamp-shire he said. He said it was everyone. All of them after you. Every organized crime outfit in the country. Which one of them killed my family?"

"I don't know."

I heard the rushing waterfall sound of blood in my ears and my vision swam because when the unvarnished truth hits, it hits like a fucking hammer. Screw that. It runs you over like a truck.

"I don't do charity," I said, and I swear the words weren't mine.

His eyes narrowed in contempt and he sniffed, a bubble of snot threatening to burst from one nostril. "Sean told me you get paid to kill people," and the name hurt us both where it hung in the air, a furious ghost refusing to depart.

He fished something from his back pocket, chair creaking alarmingly beneath his weight as he shifted, and then a stack of bills arced across the space between us. Everyone throwing money at me today. I caught the money from reflex, still reeling from the name of my friend because that's what we'd been, no matter my cowardice and denial. The wad was an inch thick, held together by two rubber bands.

"A grand plus twenty-one," he said, and I put it down beside my hip on the rumpled blanket.

I laughed and let it be cruel. He didn't want this on him. No one did. "You fucking amateur," I said and my lips curled in disdain. "I don't get outta bed for less than ten large."

"Lisa said you'd do it for whatever I had. That's what I got."

"Lisa doesn't know shit. You don't want this," I said. "You do not want to carry this much weight."

"Fuckin' coward," he surged up, chair toppling behind him. He held out a meaty hand, face screwed up like a child trying not to weep in front of the other kids. "Gimme my goddamned money, I gotta buy a gun."

I stood, flicking the money behind me onto the pillows, message clear. He'd have to go through me. His eyes slitted and he sucked in a breath, ready to do just that.

Jesus, I couldn't hit this kid again. Not after what I'd done to his family. The money was a joke if I thought about it as payment. Took me a moment to realize what it was. Honor. He needed skin in the game.

What I'd told him about charity was true. But this wasn't that kind of work, not my usual work.

This was a debt I owed.

"Five bucks a head," I said and tried to calculate it but couldn't. "Here." I handed him the hotel stationary that had once held my death note. A pen. "Do the math."

He took a knee beside the table and set to work on his long division, tongue sticking from the side of his mouth. I wondered what grade he'd made it to before he dropped out.

Claws clicked on the exposed hallway outside and padded into the room. I felt the presence of my dog and didn't need to look to know what color it was. Which dog would cut and run and which would charge into the teeth of Hell?

"Two hundred and four point two," Number Four said.

"Round it up."

"Supposed to round it down if it's below point five," he said, and I decided he'd reached a higher grade than I ever did.

"Humor me."

"Two hundred and five."

I crossed to the window sill and picked up the box of 9mm rounds. A working man's bullets. The best kind for my gun.

I would need more.

My back was to him as I grabbed the Glock and ejected the magazine. I opened the cardboard lid of the box and began loading rounds, pressing them down against a stiff spring with my thumb.

"I will bring you two hundred and five heads," I told him, sliding the full clip into the butt of the weapon and seating it with an efficient click. "The Italians. Chinese. Japanese. Russians. All of them will bleed."

I looked at him and even in the gloom I could pull every detail from the shadows. He blanched at the sight of my eyes but nodded, muscles in his neck tight, no longer weeping.

"I'll start here."

TWENTY-THREE

- 1 -

"I ain't going."

"Go home."

"Fuck you, I'm staying."

"Fuck you you are."

"Fuck you."

"Leave."

"Fuck you."

"You're baggage. You're useless. I can't use you."

"Fuck—"

I jabbed my finger deep into the meat of Number Four's chest and got in his face. His breath stank of onions and ketchup.

"You want these assholes dead, or is this about getting your prick wet?"

"What?"

Ten minutes later I was on the sidewalk watching his brake lights flash before he took a right turn, heading for Route 3 south to Boston. His home.

"That was mean," Lisa said.

"Yeah."

She looked at the corner, then at me. "Yeah. What about Ava?"

The name rolled over me in a wave as if it carried mystical force. A word of power to conjure me by. Lisa saw it and looked away.

"I don't know," I said.

"Yeah."

- 2 -

The restaurant was a noisy, two-level place made from a hollowed-out river mill, all red brick on the outside and bright lights, piñatas and sombreros on the inside. The place was called Margaritas, and that's what we were drinking at tall tables out on a wooden deck standing on stilts over the water. It was a girly drink without much knockout power, but at least the tremble had left my hands. I decided I'd ask the waitress to skip the salted rim and double the tequila on the next round.

The Glock was wrapped inside my new leather jacket on an empty seat beside me.

It was going on eight and I could see the lights come alive on Nashua's Main Street. The occasional bird flying overhead was reduced to a passing shadow and a busboy came around each table lighting candles in round, colored globes. Even outside I could smell baked corn chips and cilantro, and my tongue tasted of salt. The river offered a faint whisper from beneath us, and passing cars added a muted growl. Cheerful music and the metal clink of silverware were omnipresent beneath the cacophony of voices and laughter.

Several girls at the next table did a round of shots and laughed, cheering and coughing as they picked up limes and took a ritual bite. Life was always strangely colored when I crawled out of the hole, but this time was different. Everything edged in silver like a cloud trying and failing to conceal the moon. Sounds tinkled like wind chimes.

"Can I take your order?" the waitress asked, pretty and short with dark hair in a braid.

"Yo quiero dos tacos," Lisa said. "Al pastor, por favor."

"Grathias," the girl replied and Lisa smiled, earning a smile in return.

"You're from Spain?" Lisa asked.

"Brazil," the girl said. "But I did my undergraduate studies in Madrid."

Another round of cheers erupted from the table of girls nearby, and I glanced over to see a grinning waiter pouring a round of shots. I was trying to count the number of people on the deck. Get a feel for how many people two hundred and five looked like. Grace was right. I worked alone and up close. Line 'em up and knock 'em down. The odds of doing that two hundred and five times in a row without eating a bullet were slim.

"I'm sorry," the waitress said, touching the back of my hand to get my attention. "Can I get you another margarita?"

"Yeah. Skip the salt but put in more tequila, all right?"

"I'll bring you a Cadillac."

"Make that two," Lisa said and tipped her glass to finish the last of her drink.

When the waitress left Lisa propped her elbows behind her on the chair. "This place is nice."

I could see faint beads of perspiration on her forehead and the hollow of her throat, and I wiped a line of sweat off my upper lip. Mariachi music was piped outside over speakers. I was playing absently with the line of lights strung along the railing beside me. They were green and red and shaped vaguely like jalapeños by someone who'd never seen a pepper.

Lisa pulled a pack of Chesterfields from her purse, lighting one from the matchbook the restaurant placed in each table's ashtray. "You owe the kid," she said through a cloud of smoke.

"He can't be much younger than you are."

She shrugged.

"What do you think I owe you?" I asked.

Her eyes went flinty and her chin dropped like a boxer expecting a punch. "Nothing." She stubbed out her cigarette, lips thinning. "You walked out on me once. Do it again and I won't come after you." She smiled, but the twist of her lips had miles to go before it could reach her eyes and it died, starved of humor long before it got there. "Pops used to tell me I was stupid. He was right. Takes me a few times to get the message."

I felt sick and not from the hangover, buying myself a little time to brush sweat from my forehead when the waitress returned with our drinks. She must have felt that the air was heavy with more than the heat because she left without any chatter.

"You still thinking about her?"

"No," I took an angry sip of the margarita, suddenly aware of how ridiculous the gesture was. "Shit."

"That would have looked better with a shot." She read my mind. "How're you gonna do it?"

"Invite everyone to dinner and give them food poisoning."

She sipped her drink and licked salt from her upper lip before asking, "Really?"

"No." I dipped a finger into my margarita and pressed an ice cube beneath the surface. "I need equipment."

"I can—"

"I need help, but you need to know what you're getting into."

"They were my family too."

I looked into her eyes, waiting for her to break contact. When she held onto my gaze I said, "Let me tell you about the Townie Mafia."

TWENTY-FOUR

- 1 -

The hanging metal cage of a bug zapper flashed with blue electricity and a squadron of the blood-drinking fliers died, but the mosquitoes were as endless as the stars overhead and I worried we'd bleed out beside the double-wide.

"Ever notice how any place named Hills is wicked ugly?" Slap. Lisa hunkered lower in the passenger seat and rubbed at the bloody smear of a dead bug on her shoulder. We were both sweating from the muggy heat, smoking, bored, irritated.

"Beverly Hills is nice," I said.

"Whatever."

"Playboy Mansion is in Holmby Hills."

"Well, Baboosic Hills sucks."

True. Baboosic Hills was a trailer park and we'd followed a police car into its cramped streets. The cruiser was squatting in the driveway of a rusting trailer down the road, parked beside a weed-choked yard littered with toys. A dog barked somewhere in the distance and I heard a woman yelling, maybe on TV. None of the cars in the driveways of Baboosic Hills were of recent vintage, and the best of the vehicles was a tow truck, cursive signage on the side panel declaring that it was owner operated.

"I don't think they teach kids cursive anymore," Lisa said.

Most of the yards were well-tended but a few, like the one we were parked beside, were spiky and overgrown with yellow grass. Those grasses occasionally twitched like the hide of a wild animal in mid-dream and I wondered if there were cats or rats hunting in the night.

"Dammit," Lisa cursed and killed another insect. We had briefly tried rolling up the windows but the heat and stink of perfume quickly overwhelmed us.

"Notice how every car has its own smell?" Lisa . She opened the glove compartment and pulled out a couple plastic clamshell hair clips. "Office girl, still in her twenties. She leaves the house with her hair wet and sprays on perfume when she drives to work."

I grunted.

The trailer's door opened with a screech, and an outdoor light snapped on to reveal screens threaded liberally with the flaking bodies of dead moths. A police officer in a light-blue shirt and dark-blue slacks descended the metal steps and stood by his cruiser. He was big but stoop-shouldered, his belly hanging over his belt. The woman was no more than a vague shape in the doorway, and I couldn't hear what they said.

"She blew him," Lisa said.

"How do you know?"

"He gels his hair back," she said. "If he fucked her, he'd have messed it up. He'd be touching it if he just gelled it back into place."

"Huh," I said, not caring all that much if some lady got out of a speeding ticket with a blow job. I stubbed out my cigarette in a Dunkin' Donuts cup and my shakes weren't too bad, but I needed a beer to settle my stomach, still a little off from my last tumble down the hole.

"He looks like an asshole," she said.

I leaned down to reconnect the wires beneath the steering column.

"He married?" Lisa asked.

"Not last time I saw him."

"Think she's married?"

I pictured the toys in the yard, driveway empty of any other vehicle. The husband probably had the family car, working third shift somewhere, his family hanging on by the fingernails.

"Doesn't seem right," Lisa said as if I'd answered.

"Nope," I said as I sparked the engine to life. It was an old Honda and didn't sound like much, but I suspected it would run another twenty years.

"Is it smart to follow a cop?" Lisa asked as we eased out. I waited until our quarry's red taillights turned right onto the two-lane main road before I flicked on the Honda's low beams.

"Cop's just a guy like everyone else."

"Yeah but…"

"No buts."

We slowed at the intersection and eased into a right turn but rolled over the sandy shoulder by accident. Towering pines crowded the road and a narrow band of stars shone overhead. As we cruised past thirty miles per hour the breeze rushed in through the windows and Lisa straightened up, plucking the sweaty tank top away from her chest. A rumbling lumber truck blew by going the opposite way and as his headlights flooded the Honda I stole a glance at Lisa, her skin shining and wet.

"Why do we want this guy?" she asked as I depressed the dashboard lighter. She produced another butt for me without asking and stuck it in my mouth. "Why do we want him?" she repeated and I spoke around the cigarette in my lips.

"He's the corner I'm gonna peel up."

- 2 -

A couple of pickup trucks and muscle cars were parked in the gravel lot, pulled up to a long, low building made to look like a log cabin with a slanting, tin roof. Two Harleys sat beneath the sodium lamp on a wooden light pole, moths darting up toward the artificial sun. A hand-painted wooden sign by the side of the road named the place HOWARD'S TRADING POST, though the side of the building dedicated to trading was dark.

"What is it, Tuesday?"

"Yeah," she said.

"You know what to do?"

"Yeah."

I'd already smashed the dome light so I didn't give much away when I pushed my door open and jogged into the brush beside the road. I had on my leather jacket to ward off the mosquitoes and was streaming sweat by the time I crouched against the base of a tree.

Lisa crawled over the gearshift, took my place, and pulled the Honda into a spot a few cars away from the police cruiser.

I could hear her heavy boots grinding through the gravel and a rush of music when she opened the door to go inside.

The smell of beer wafted to me from the bar, and I grew wetter and wetter in my leather jacket and jeans, steaming like a fish cooked in a banana leaf. My stomach rumbled with hunger and I wanted a cigarette, but didn't want to give myself away so I counted instead, keeping a loose watch on the door to Howard's.

I tried bracing a knee on the soft carpet of pine needles but slipped and ended up just sitting against the hard bark, tree sap be damned. My left hand slid over something fleshy that felt like an ear and broke beneath my palm. I hoped it was a mushroom. I thought about Daniel Day Lewis in *The Last of the Mohicans* and wondered what this forest was like before the white man came and fucked it up.

When I reached three hundred and eighty-nine, having lost my place only twice, the door opened and Lisa strode outside in a spill of light and music.

She climbed into the Honda and slammed the door, revving the engine for a moment before she cranked the radio, the sound fuzzy and indistinct from my vantage point.

"Don't push it," I muttered.

The door opened and the bulky silhouette of our quarry filled the space as she backed out of her spot and eased out of the parking lot.

I was already running in the ditch separating the shoulder from the trees and she cruised past, keeping it slow.

The police car was on her almost immediately, the driver not feeling any need for subtlety. Spitting out sand where I lay on my belly,

I wondered how many people in this burg knew that a fuck or a suck would get a ticket torn up. I reflected on the nature of small towns and the crimes they concealed while I caught my breath.

The cop pulsed his roof lights and Lisa pulled over so I pushed myself back into a trot. A flash of the cruiser's dome light as he emerged and then his shape was looming over the small Honda. She turned on her interior light to give him a look and play hell with his night vision, like we discussed. I imagined their conversation as the breath burned in my lungs and my boots slipped and thudded toward them. She'd downed a shot of tequila right in front of him, after all. Downed a shot and got behind the wheel. "Have you been drinking, ma'am?" He'd be polite at first. Testing the water, wondering if he'd actually have to bust her for a DUI instead of getting a look at her tits.

He looked up just as I swarmed out of the ditch and his eyes had a chance to widen, his lips to stretch back off his teeth before the butt of my pistol met his nose and he went down.

I stomped hard on his balls and he curled into a fetal position, blurting out something I didn't care about as I grabbed his shirt collar and jerked him around until I could club him behind the ear with the pistol, mussing his carefully coiffed hair.

Lisa was already rolling away in the Honda while I cuffed him and dragged him into the back seat of the cruiser. He was kind enough to leave the keys in the ignition and I cranked the big engine to life, rolling down the window against the odor of cabbage, grease and stale beer. I thought about the woman at the trailer park sucking his cock to escape being arrested by a guy who was probably three sheets to the wind when he pulled her over.

I understood Lisa's anger a little better.

He was moaning, "Fuck I am?" and thrashing quietly by the time I caught up to Lisa and crossed the double yellow lines to pass her on the left. She flashed her high beams once in acknowledgment and followed us as I tried to remember the route to his house.

My passenger had been making mushy sounds for a few minutes before he sat up and made himself clearer. "Do you know who the fuck I am?"

"You're Dale Hardcastle," I told him and looked at him in the rearview mirror. With the Roy Batty hair and the muttonchops, he didn't recognize me.

"How do you know my name?" he whispered, deflating like a stuck balloon.

"Dale," I said and his head whipped around as if slapped.

"W-what?"

"Who am I?"

"I don't know and I don't wanna know."

"Dale?"

"Yeah?"

"Remember Alicia Tromblay?"

I favored him with a glance over the shoulder and his eyes widened, seeing through my disguise.

"Oh shit." An acrid odor filled the air as he pissed himself.

I remembered Alicia Tromblay.

TWENTY-FIVE

- 1 -

Alicia Tromblay drank and smoked and drove a VW Bug she called the Shoe because, "It looks like a baby's shoe."

"I still can't believe you're doing this," Mim said, shivering despite the hot air blowing from the heater. She didn't like the strange way the orange dashboard lights illuminated her friend's face, all shadows and glimmering pools of fire. The toddler-sized shoe dangling from the rearview mirror—a black and white Mary Jane—was strangely menacing.

"Number seven, Whopper Jr. combo," Alicia said into the drive-through microphone before turning to Mim in the passenger seat. "It's been two years since UNH and I've moved two towns over. At this rate I won't even reach Vermont until I'm fifty."

They were both young and of a type, loose clothes and a bit out of shape, Alicia smoking a cigarette and wearing bangly earrings beneath pageboy hair, Mim wearing a gold peace sign in her left ear, hair cut close in a blonde skull cap.

Alicia nudged the car forward and rolled up her window with the hand crank, leaving a narrow crack through which her smoke could escape. She shifted the VW into Neutral and yanked the parking brake.

"I thought you were gonna take this to the paper?" Mim asked, nervously tugging at a beaded necklace.

"Know what a starting reporter at the *New Hampshire Union Leader* makes?" Alicia shook her head and her earrings tinkled as her heavily made-up eyes narrowed. "This is my ticket out of here."

"If it's real."

"The TM is totally real."

"Like the secret oil spill off Hampton Beach?" Mim punched her in the thigh. "If anyone actually read your blog, Unitil would've sued your ass."

Alicia favored her friend with a withering look before rolling down her window and reaching out to grab the white Burger King bag. She handed the food to Mim who stole a French fry while Alicia nursed the car out of the parking lot and onto the poorly lit road, careful of the ice.

"Hey!" Alicia complained.

Mim produced another fry and stuck it in Alicia's mouth before turning up the radio. Sting was singing about Englishmen in New York.

"I'd do him," Alicia said, chewing.

"Sting?"

"He's wicked hot."

"I think it's gonna snow," Mim said as the road hissed beneath their wheels, but Alicia spoke as if she hadn't heard.

"If the Townie Mafia isn't real, how come they agreed to pay?"

- 2 -

The center of town was known locally as the Oval and passed as the small town's business district. It was a roundabout circling a small park with a white painted bandstand, flagpole and a memorial to sons lost in the Korean War. On the outside of the loop were storefronts, some towering as high as two stories.

Alicia piloted the Shoe around while Mim looked longingly at the bright lights of the House of Pizza and at clustered smokers shivering outside of the Pasta Loft, which had a live band every Thursday night.

"I don't like this," Mim said. She put down her phone after reading the article Alicia had written as a piece of investigative journalism before deciding the article presented a less savory but more financially rewarding option. "The cops are involved?"

"Just some of them," Alicia said, chain smoking to hide her own worries. "And just to transport the drugs in-state. Mostly heroin now."

"Except for the guns."

"Well, yeah. They do some stuff to clean up records of the guns from at least two different buy-back programs and the TM sells them down in Massachusetts."

"The cops are gonna find out who you are."

"It's not 'the cops.' Just some of the local guys, not even Staties." Alicia stubbed out her butt among its peers in the ashtray. "I'm using PayPal connected to a new email address. No way fuckin' Barney Fife is gonna find out who I am."

"This is so dumb."

"It's the Townie Mafia," Alicia said, cranking the volume on the radio. "Not the Cali Cartel."

- 3 -

Alicia set the half-empty bottle of Chianti back on her scarred coffee table. It was the good kind with banded straw on the outside and had a lively taste, especially after a few glasses. Several lit candles were placed around the room in similar bottles she'd emptied over the past two years.

"I'm feelin' it," Mim said as she sipped crimson nectar from a glass sporting a Thundercats decal.

It was dark outside the windows and the room was quiet, drifting with smoke from the joint pinched in Alicia's fingers and the guitar strains of Jim Croce. A tie-dyed sheet serving as a curtain fluttered over the window she'd cracked to let out the smoke.

"Shoulda eaten something," Alicia said.

"Burger King is bad for you."

It was a small room in a small house with natural wood walls and a motley collection of furniture scrounged from yard sales and her mom's basement. What decorations there were still carried the whiff of college, unframed posters and thumbtacked articles. The rugs were of the throw variety, and Alicia's TV was twenty years old, heavy and box-like.

But the fireplace was lit and emitting warmth and a scent that always comforted Alicia. *My place isn't so bad*, she thought. *Or maybe I'm a little stoned.*

"Stop worrying," Alicia said. "Those damned chickens will go ape shit if anyone sneaks up on the house." She had a coop in her backyard alongside an herb garden she planted in the spring.

"They didn't when we came in."

"Because they knew it was me."

"The chickens knew," Mim said dryly.

"Chickens are smart."

Mim reflected on the intelligence of chickens and friends alike and took another swig of Chianti. She waved at the laptop sitting open on the coffee table. "Check again."

Alicia scowled and leaned forward, tapping several keys.

"Crap."

"Shit."

Alicia giggled and Mim shook her head but couldn't hold back a tipsy grin. "This isn't funny."

Alicia stuck the joint in her teeth and pushed herself up with a puff of smoke, which almost made her laugh again. "I gotta whiz."

"TMI," Mim barked, and they both laughed as Alicia made a weaving path down the narrow hall to the bathroom, slide-walking in her socks. She nudged open the bathroom door with her knee and thought about the can of sky-blue paint she had in the garage so she could touch up the peeling exterior. "Soon, my friend," she muttered, the joint bobbing in her mouth. She plucked it from her lips and leaned over to place it carefully on the edge of the sink with her left hand while executing a ninja move—flicking the door closed with her right foot.

She grinned and hooked her thumbs in the waistband of her sweatpants, yanking them and her underwear down before she caught a reflection in the mirror, a dark man-shape over her right shoulder previously hidden behind the door.

A strong hand clenched the hair at the back of her skull and yanked down, lifting her chin skyward as a straight razor was dragged across her throat, deep enough to slice both carotids and jugular. She released a tremendous fan of ruby liquid across the wall and a loud, wet sigh from the wound. Her mouth was trying to form words when her face was shoved toward the toilet so that most of the blood would spray into the bowl.

She twitched and flopped for several long seconds before the tension left her body. The blade was wiped on a threadbare bath towel adorned with faded blue flowers before it was folded and replaced in a pocket. A moment later she was alone in the bathroom.

It was another twenty minutes before Mim thought to check on Alicia.

Her scream filled the night.

- 4 -

It was that rare enough event, a payment in person. After killing Alicia Tromblay, an unmarked Caprice met me at a deserted rest stop on Interstate 93, well after midnight. I was already in a sour mood from the killing and the need to scrounge change for the highway tollbooths. The man who emerged from the car was dressed in jeans and a blue sweatshirt, a big man but sloppily built. He walked with a cop's arrogance, though, and I knew him for what he was.

He had a long duffel bag in one freckled hand.

"Rooster," he said, planting himself in front of me where I leaned against an open-sided structure that contained vending machines.

I smoked and waited. I knew who the fuck I was.

"Anyone see you?" he asked like he made the decisions.

"You did."

I didn't smile, but after an awkward moment he did. When I still didn't say anything an emotion of a truculent nature twisted his lips and he dropped his duffel bag on the ground beside the one I'd brought with me.

"Here it is," he said, putting some muscle into his tone. "Time for you to get out of New Hampshire."

I smoked and ignored his various expressions until he decided there was no point in dragging out our chat and stomped away like a kid in a huff. A little funny looking on a biggish man like him.

His car backed out of the slot, tailpipe smoking in the cold, and coasted past my position slow, tires scraping over sand and gravel. That game had only so many outcomes, though, and he drove off after a moment.

I picked up a blue nylon hockey bag heavy with several thousand dollars worth of clean firearms, my payment, and bid adieu to New Hampshire, armpit of the northeast.

- 5 -

Lisa didn't like the story.

TWENTY-SIX

- 1 -

As soon as I left Lisa at the motel everything went to hell. One cluster-fuck after the next and we'd just reached FUBAR. Fucked up beyond all repair. Shit like this never happened in the city.

I was standing with a gun in my hand surrounded by skyscrapers of garbage, a post-apocalyptic landscape illuminated by a roaring fire. The flames cast the scene in Halloween shades of orange and black, flickering across my vision like the rippling hide of a hunting tiger. The night was made darker by clouds of toxic smoke.

"Wade, you asshole!" I shouted.

A warbling cackle bounced and echoed around me and music filled the air with psychedelia.

I spun and sighted in on a towering shadow looming over the pyramids of trash, wild scarecrow arms stretching twenty feet in each direction.

"Wade!"

This just wouldn't happen in the city.

- 2 -

A short while earlier I'd prodded a naked Dale into the woods with the business end of my gun.

He whimpered and stumbled, staggering when he cut his bare feet on branches and rocks, big belly wobbling, buttocks jiggling. When he slowed, I whispered sweet nothings and he picked up the pace.

"Y-y-you should start seeing the markers," he stammered and I stopped, bracing my hand against the rough bark of a giant pine as I traded my small flashlight for the infrared penlight in my pocket. The tip glowed like an angry e-cigarette when I depressed the button but the beam itself was invisible.

"All right," I said and stepped away from the tree, my fingers sticky with sap. I wiped them on my jeans but the viscous substance had become one with my skin. "Shit."

Smelled nice, though.

Lisa was back at the nearest Bates Motel with Dale's sidearm and clothes. His pad was a place of woodgrain paneling and shag carpets in varying shades of orange or brown and all the unwashed dishes ever dirtied piled in his sink. One look at the joint and she said she wouldn't wait there. One look at Lisa and I knew she was still processing how Dale and I had met. What we'd done.

Maybe listening to Alicia's ghost.

Dale had been naked atop a furry sea of burnt umber when Lisa walked out, and I jammed my knee into his spine, waiting for the door to close before I broke every finger on his cuffed left hand. All that shag muffled his screams.

Without much more persuading he led me behind his house into the muggy confines of the old pine forest, towering trees blocking out the stars overhead while here and there a white birch pointed skyward like a pale finger, all knuckles and bones. It was jungle hot, ninety degrees even after sunset. Dale's body glimmered with a greasy sheen of sweat, and I could feel steaming rivers of perspiration trickling down my own ribs and pooling at the base of my spine. I licked salt from my upper lip and stole a sip of cheap whiskey from a flask I borrowed from Dale's kitchen. A shifting cloud of mosquitoes and black flies feasted on my prisoner but stayed away from me, unable to penetrate the leather jacket or the cloud of smoke from the Chesterfield clamped in my teeth.

"What's that?" I nudged something big, square and metal up with my toe and let it fall back with a *whumpf*. The number 55 was spray-painted atop it.

"Car hood," Dale offered.

"In the middle of the woods?"

Dale shrugged.

Every few steps I played the infrared beam across the trees in front of us as we wound among the boles, looking for a bright flash of infrared paint to guide our way. Branches whipped the bare skin of my prisoner and his knees were bloody from repeated falls, but other than his incessant whimpering, he offered no protest. High-pitched squeaks nearly past my ability to hear accompanied flapping overhead. Bats maybe. I thought about asking Dale but he was pretty focused on staying alive and I didn't want to distract him.

We were surprisingly quiet as we moved over the bed of pine needles on the forest floor, and the absence of car sounds and distant radio voices was eerie. Out among the trees it felt as if the age of man had passed on by, the buildings fallen, the airwaves silent. A century after the big war.

But I was just in New Hampshire.

Even through my boots I felt the trail before I made out its edges in the gloom and the deep ruts churned by dirt bikes. We followed the path and the going was a little easier until I picked up another infrared flash to my right and cajoled Dale in that direction.

Even over my cigarette I picked up the smell, an enticing aroma from a wood fire layered over something uglier. Something sweet and rotting and huge.

Dale risked a glance back at me and I saw a bubble of snot expand in his right nostril. I gave the chubby asshole a shove and we stepped from the trees into the open beneath a star-spangled sky. He stumbled to a stop at the edge of a steep cliff and knocked a beer can over the side. The dead soldier tumbled and bounced down into the ugliest valley in the world. America's graveyard.

"Damn, Dale. The town dump?"

- 3 -

Hiding weapons and drugs in a dump displayed a certain kind of brilliance. Particularly when those doing the hiding owned the local officials. But what I said was, "Of course you fucking hillbillies hide gear in the dump. Trash calls to trash, am I right?"

We were squatting beside a pyramid of stacked refrigerators, the doors removed for safety and piled nearby. Dale's head dropped lower on his neck and I looked away, almost ashamed for him. Guy felt like Genghis Khan only a few hours ago, sticking his dick into some housewife's mouth. The worm turns, bitch. The worm turns.

I stood with a loud crack from both knees and wished I'd remembered to bring more Tylenol. "You sure no one's coming by tonight?"

"They only schedule deliveries or pickups when I'm on duty so I can run interference," Dale said in something below a mumble.

"Just this guy Wade in there?"

"Just Wade."

"Get up."

He struggled up without my help and I scanned the area again with deliberate care. The good stuff was piled closer to the custodian's shack. Electronics. Engine parts. Clothes. The shack itself was a shabby structure with tarpaper walls and plastic sheeting covering lopsided windows. A fire blazed on the far side of the structure, big enough that I could see the sparks rising over the roof. The dirt here was well churned with tire tracks, a busy spot during the day. Easy to slip in and out to take care of something less than legal using the square Johns for cover.

A certain kind of smart.

I leaned close and rested my chin on Dale's sweaty shoulder. He flinched but didn't bolt. Up close he smelled worse than the dump. "You give old Wade any kind of warning and I'll cut your balls off while you're still breathing. Make you chew them. Swallow them before you bleed out. Nod if you understand."

He bleated, the sound a farm animal might make, but nodded hurriedly. I made a kissing sound next to his ear. "Good boy. You keep thinking good-boy thoughts and get me what I want, you'll live through this night."

"Th-thank y—"

I rapped the back of his head with the gun butt and he flinched but shut up.

"Now move."

We were angled so as to approach one of the four corners of the shack, where a humming refrigerator stood next to the only door. My guess was it contained half a case of Budweiser, though Miller High Life was not out of the question. If ever a place demanded the Champagne of Beers, it was the Baboosic Town Dump.

When we reached the corner, I grabbed Dale's neck and lightly kicked the back of his knee, easing him down onto his haunches. I held a finger across my smile before I placed my back against the wall and inched forward until I could sneak a look through the window.

I had a blurry view of the spartan interior and saw a cot strewn with blankets, a rebuilt wooden bookshelf and a desk made from a closet door placed across sawhorses. Another set of shelves featured partially reconstructed toys, heavily armed robots for the most part, and a wheelbarrow was stacked with old nudie magazines. Artwork on the walls was divided evenly between fading centerfolds and official-looking papers with state seals.

Wade was seated at the desk with his back to me, so thin that the bumps of his spine stood out like knots and his shoulder blades looked sharp enough to pierce the skin. He was a gangly creature with buzz cut hair, tall even sitting, and there was some kind of cyst on the side of his neck.

I moved for a better view and saw that his right arm was pistoning furiously. I realized he was looking at a laptop computer.

Worked for me.

Dale made a good battering ram and the door wasn't much so we were through quickly. I let Dale fall to his knees at Wade's feet. The dump custodian sprang up from his chair and almost tripped over the green Dickies bunched around his ankles. His eyes went wide and he threw his hands up, but that defiant cock was pointed at me like a challenge to joust.

"I want the guns and the money, Wade," I said, leveling the Glock at his left eye. "You give me both and I'll be gone before you lose that hard-on."

His pinched face dipped to look down at me, nearly comical in his shock. He had long, terrible teeth that may have been filed for sharpness, and his eyes were glazed with something that came in pill form. "You got it, buddy," he said in a weird, high-pitched voice, a childish sound that didn't match the scarecrow body. He kicked the pants off his right foot and then the left before I could tell him to pull them up, and then he gestured to the door with a sweep of his bruised arm. "This way, boss."

- 4 -

I followed behind Wade's bony ass and Dale's flabbier example as we circled around the blazing trash fire.

"I've got this here enormous Johnson but none of the ladies will fuck me because I work in a dump," Wade said in his piping voice, strutting along with a jaunty bounce to his never-ending erection. He said *fook me* like an Irishman. "Everything I wear I cull from the dump," he'd said proudly, pointing to the green Adidas on his feet, his only clothing. "Guardin' this place is a dream job once you get used to the smell."

"Guarding," Dale snorted, summoning a little spirit at last.

Wade favored his shuffling, barefooted friend with a sad expression. "It's an Achilles heel for sure," he said and glanced back at me. "I've got to masturbate at least eight or ten times a day or I can't concentrate on anything."

Dale stumbled and hopped with a curse. "I'm gonna get an infection," he whined, and I almost shot him there. He read the lack of sympathy in my eyes and resumed his dogged march, but I could hear him muttering.

"Don't you talk yourself into being a man now, Dale," I said to his back. "I only need one of you to dig up the stuff."

"You only need me, actually," Wade suggested. "Shoot Dale and I won't tell."

"Shut up," Dale hissed.

"It's true, boyo," Wade said.

"Shut *up*."

Wade stopped at an open space and planted his fists on his hips, turning to face me and still alarmingly erect. I wondered if he was crazy before he took the job, or lost his mind after spending too much time in this place.

"Here it is, boss." He pointed at the ground and dragged the toe through the dirt to reveal the edge of a board. He walked toward a stack of broken furniture.

I took aim on his spine and said, "Easy there." But he raised his hands and crouched, then lifted a dirt-covered chain with a combination lock on it.

"You got a weapon hidden here, Wade?"

"Yep."

"Dale, you work the combination. Wade, tell him."

I stepped behind Dale and undid his handcuffs and he clutched his wounded hand with a cry of relief, fresh streams of sweat running down his face. The fingers were purple now and thicker than polish sausages. He'd lose them if he didn't see a doctor soon.

"C'mere, Wade."

"Oh, now that's—"

"Knock it off." I tossed him the cuffs and he locked his own hands in front of his body while Dale knelt next to the combination lock.

Wade said, "Turn it three times to the right to seventeen…"

Two minutes later I swore. "Dale. You fuck this up again and Wade's gonna do it because you won't have a head."

"Boss, one question," Wade said, and the humor left his speech, his piping voice as serious as it could be. "Do you know who you're fuckin' with?"

Fookin.

Dale slapped Wade's knee and shook his head, whispering something I couldn't hear.

"What?" I asked.

Dale looked at me with stark terror and Wade with dawning appreciation. He smiled like a man receiving a cancer diagnosis.

"He said that you're the guy on the website." Wade's prominent Adam's apple bobbed up and down as he swallowed. His fishbelly-white skin was clammy as his high faded. "Killer everyone's after. One they call the Rooster."

Hearing from Grace that everyone up and down the criminal food chain was looking for me was one thing, but hearing it from this gutter slime was reality on another level. The unfamiliar chill of fear gripped my middle and the sweat went cold on my body.

"Tell me about the website." My knuckles went white around the pistol grip.

"Don't, boss," Wade said and held his hands out, pleading.

"It's done," Dale said and tossed aside the combination lock. He stood and grabbed the chain in one hand and gave a big jerk, pulling aside a plywood section maybe eight feet on a side. A small landslide of dirt slid down into the dark hole but my flashlight glinted off metal and I could smell the sharp tang of gun oil.

"Good—" I started, then Wade kneed Dale in the head and the big cop tumbled into the hole. Wade spun away with awkward speed and ducked around the stack of furniture. He slapped at a lever only he could see and an entire section of trash tumbled between us.

I sent two rounds cracking after him and jumped down into the hole, a ten-foot drop that knocked me to my knees. I lost the flashlight but moonlight revealed Dale in all his glory, and I put a bullet into him before standing.

He was writhing like a pale grub in the dirt, clutching at the black crude oil pumping from his body. I think he was going to say something, maybe blame Wade, but I shot him through the mouth and cut short the conversation.

"Shit," I said when I scooped up my light and saw several racks of rifles secured by a chain. I ran to the ladder leaning against a wall and braced it against the opening. I climbed quickly with a lot of noise, hoping the gangly sonofabitch hadn't already found a sniper rifle.

Scrambling into the surface world I caught the sound of Wade's mad laughter echoing from the east. Thrumming filled the air and hackles rose on my neck when I recognized the strains of "White Rabbit" booming all around me as if the entire dump was wired with hidden speakers.

This place was madness made real and Wade was the Pied Piper, playing me toward him.

My flask was near empty so I finished the burning nectar and dropped it at my feet. I popped the mag of my Glock and saw six rounds. I slapped it back in and racked the slide. An entire armory was waiting below my feet, but I didn't have time to liberate it before this insane, priapic fuck came after me. Six rounds would have to do.

Whiskey fed the heat inside me and I walked toward the bonfire, my mind swirling with Mad Hatter thoughts.

- 5 -

Burning crosses lit the range of trash mountains as I stalked Wade through flowing rivers of smoke. The drugs were getting to me and I coughed, tying my sweat-soaked T-shirt over my nose and mouth to reduce their effect and slinging the leather jacket back on over my bare torso. Still, my mind wandered, sucked toward the gravitational pull of Wade's insanity, wondering what ugly fusion of madness and narcotics fueled his twisted creativity.

Movement to my right. I pivoted and dropped to one knee to reduce myself as a target, firing a single round at shifting shadows cast by yet another blaze. Light streaked across my field of vision and hung in the air in an impossible, pyrotechnic display.

I squeezed my eyes shut to banish the fiery streak and heard the clatter of debris. An avalanche of boards careened across the space I had just abandoned.

He had yet to fire a single shot but had triggered booby trap after booby trap while I pursued him deeper into the waste.

A wooden snap, sharp over the distorted music, and an object trailing green flames arced the sky to slam into a mound far behind me, igniting a trash pile pre-soaked in kerosene. Over the sharp tang of the fuel I caught the sweet scent of ganja. He had some kind of catapult rigged up out of my line of sight and was firing trash bags loaded with newspaper and marijuana laced with god knew what.

There was as much farce as murder in the moment, but I coughed through my urge toward his wild laughter. Wade had devolved into a demented, six-foot-five Macauley Culkin, rigging the entirety of the dump with homemade traps and devices. His sick brain shifting between speeds like a record player, from 33 to 45 to 78 with no apparent rhyme or reason.

I spit and cursed when saliva dribbled down the cloth over my mouth, barking a stoned laugh at the absurdity. The music ended and heavy guitars filled the silence as yet another cover of "White Rabbit" dopplered out from the speakers.

I scanned the ground ahead of me for tiger pits as another wooden cross flared alight atop a garbage pile. I had no idea what the symbolism meant to the madman, only that they created a shifting, rippling landscape alive with false movement, and I had only five rounds left in the magazine. After that I'd have to spend precious minutes reloading it with loose rounds from the pocket of my jacket.

Fluting notes came to me and I realized Wade was shouting, but the words were unintelligible.

"You're insane!" I shouted back and triggered a laughing jag. Me? Him? I wasn't sure.

My arrival had triggered Wade's DefCon One scenario. The event he had been building toward since the TM first stationed him here.

A string of firecrackers made a racket to my left and I moved right out of instinct, jerking to a halt as another trash fall sent burning automobile tires bouncing across my path. The bang of the catapult echoed and an orange meteor flew across my horizon. I fired at a shape silhouetted against the flames and blew the head off a naked mannequin.

Four rounds remaining.

Events were occurring faster now, building to a fireworks crescendo. Dozens of man-made mountaintops were alight with burning crosses as trap after trap triggered. I knew I should run, abandon the plan, but I was disoriented by the narcotic smoke and herded by the bizarre attacks.

Another string of firecrackers popped off and I lifted my knees, pumping my arms as I broke into a desperate sprint toward the central bonfire.

It happened fast. My boot punched through a thin cover, the heavy soles crushing several wooden stakes jutting up from below. I rolled away, cursing, batting with my pistol at a sharpened stick stuck into the cuff of my jeans as a Molotov cocktail exploded nearby. I threw up my arm against the flames, feeling the heat on my face.

His charge was silent, eyes shining and round, long teeth bared in a grin. He had added a tool belt holding knives and a hammer but was otherwise naked save for his shoes. Whorls of dark mud covered his white skin and his ever-present erection bounced with every step. He clutched a revolver in one hand and began firing, the shots wild, but I flinched and my return fire missed. When I tried to aim from my back, he yanked the hammer from his belt and hurled it at me. The weapon spun end over end and I threw my arms up in an X, the blow jarring as the hammer bounced aside.

Then he was on me.

It was like battling the incoming tide. A storm. He was swinging knives in both hands and kicking, then dropping his knees on my gut. All without blinking. Without losing that wild grin.

I blocked the knives and ate the knee. Grunting, my injured ribs screaming as I used the tough leather sleeves of the motorcycle jacket to sweep the blades aside. I locked my legs around his hips, looping my left arm behind his head to yank his nose down against mine. He turned his face as I bit so I tore a chunk of cartilage from his ear and drove hooking punches into the back of his skull until he couldn't stand it and jerked back. I used his momentum and jammed my boot heels against his thighs, kicking him off me and twisting, rolling away and up to my feet.

My right ankle buckled and I fell to one knee.

Wade flew at me like a great kite of white flesh and I caught him, torquing my hips to slam his shoulders against the dirt as I slithered atop him and locked my hands on his Adam's apple.

He spit a wad of white powder in my face.

"Fuck!"

I reared back and he shoved me off as I tried to stand, weak ankle giving way, desperately wiping clumps of white from blurring eyes and spitting it from a tongue gone numb.

His laughter warbled, wavering like the music as the chemicals fought for the reigns of my perceptions and won.

Wade rose to an impossible height, shifting like the viscous blob in a lava lamp. He was singing in fuzzy, underwater tones and I was falling...

"Feed your head!"

And falling...

"Feed your head!"

Falling...

"Feed your head!"

- 6 -

"Fuck you, Nancy Reagan. Drug use saved my life!"

I don't think I said this out loud, though my memory of shouting at the former First Lady on the set of the Maury Povich Show is crystal clear.

My front pocket was vibrating and I mumbled something about Dale needing to answer his phone since it was in my pocket, right around the time I felt a distant pain in my shoulders and noticed the ground sliding beneath the seat of my pants and the heels of my boots.

Sizzling drops of saliva fell like wet meteors from Wade's upside-down horror mask and burned craters in the skin of my face. I was being dragged. The music was still playing, and my mouth tasted like an old shoe.

Thank god for years of drug abuse and a well-developed tolerance. My system was kicking out the PCP or heroin or whatever the hell it was.

Dale was dead.

I was alive.

Wade was dragging me through the dump.

I jerked both of my hands toward my shoulders and thumped down against the dirt. The glassy eyed Irishman stooped to grab me and I jacked my left knee up hard into the crown of his skull. He bounced out of my line of sight.

"Sonofa—" I rolled to my hands and knees as Wade sat up holding his skull. Pushing myself upright and gritting my teeth against the pain in my ankle I booted him in the teeth with a satisfying crack. Blood sprayed from his mouth in a Pollock display and he went back, generously exposing scrotum. He howled when I stomped, curling around himself like a convulsing shrimp.

I staggered and spit and vomited, in that order, before making out the wooden cross of roped-together four-by-fours surrounded by a makeshift pyre of rubber tires.

"Fuck you!" I snarled, my fury molten with the sluggish heat of lava meeting cold air. I hooked a hand beneath his armpit, ignoring the ringing phone in my pocket and coughing against the smoke from the hellscape around me.

A mismatched set of handcuffs were affixed to the waiting cross and I pushed Wade against the thick pole, fighting against him to manacle first his right hand and then his left to the crossbar.

He was screaming and kicking but my ears were still stuffed with cotton, his speaker system too close as it banged out Jefferson Airplane's hallucinogenic anthem on an endless loop and I laughed at the naked, crazy fuck when I picked up the sloshing can of kerosene and gave him a golden shower with the contents.

"You're limp!" Laughing at his finally flaccid cock, I spat at him and scooped up a burning torch from the nearest mountain of shit before I set old Wade on fire.

His scream was a thing of beauty.

"DIE MOTHERFUCKER!" I howled at him, maybe not so shed of the drugs after all and laughing, throwing things at the writhing man while his skin blackened and split to expose white ribs amidst pink meat. I drank in the delicious odor of roasting pork and vomited against my appetite. Hearing the sirens then. Knowing that dead Dale's phone was ringing because the TM was screaming, "What the hell is going on?"

I scooped up a revolver from the ground and lurched away until I tumbled into the dump's glory hole. Two shots destroyed two padlocks and I found bags to stuff with rifles and slick, greasy weapons of foreign make. There were crates with banana magazines and grenades packed in straw and curved devices with stamped lettering that read: Front Toward Enemy. And cash money, good old American greenbacks wrapped in plastic-shrouded bricks.

Two duffel bags full of death I dragged from that place as sirens drew closer and vehicles swarmed like honeybees toward the edge of the dump. I pulled my hoard in the opposite direction, pausing only at Wade's shack to steal his laptop computer before climbing a dirt cliff. My boots dug great furrows in the dirt as the weight of my loot tried to pull me down, but I reached the forest floor on my hands and knees, grunting when a thick tree root punched my battered ribs.

The drugs were still singing psalms in my bloodstream and I was Hansel calling Gretel on dead Dale's cell phone. I couldn't go back to his house for the car. Couldn't drive anyway. Laughter trailed in my wake and whatever else moved in the night gave me wide berth.

"Gretel? Gretel?"

I bled and suffered and cried and remember very little of that journey, marching and crawling like a beast. I believe I spoke to the darkness without and within and the truth was nothing ever meant to be spoken by the tongue of man or heard by his ears.

Black dog and yellow dog howling in the night.

It was Lisa who found me in a ditch by the road, her face stark with fear at my ravings as she manhandled me into the backseat of a car and piled the instruments of death across me.

"Hold on," she whispered and I felt the car rocking as it pulled out with a scream of rubber.

"Hold on!"

- 7 -

She held me until my mind stitched itself back together. When this was done, I laid my plans.

TWENTY-SEVEN

- 1 -

After Lisa pulled me out of the dump, we were in the latest in the endless series of motel rooms, sweating in New Hampshire's brutal summer heat, the damn air conditioner blowing out warm air. I was just out of the shower. She was at the uneven desk.

"John?"

"Yeah?"

"You need to see this website."

"You have a laptop?"

"You brought it back from the dump."

"What's on it?"

"It names you."

"What?"

"Richard Harvest."

Heat lightning crackled across my naked body and my sweat boiled to steam.

- 2 -

The boy in the black-and-white photo pressed his lips together tight enough to drive the blood from them. His hair was a self-cut mess of jackstraws, his eyes narrowed.

He didn't look tough, he looked scared. Twelve years old and headed for reform school, he should be.

Richard "Rick" Harvest. Address unknown. No living relatives. Ward of the state. Fuck that. Prisoner.

I remembered.

There were black-and-white pictures of the school, a blocky, three-story building in the outskirts of the Bronx. The lack of color didn't show the oxidation on the chain-link fence, but I could remember the way it smelled and the taste of rust still lived on my tongue. The teachers taught with their fists, but I learned my most important lessons from the other students. Boys my age with stories written in scars and cigarette burns and hate.

My breath was coming in small sips and the air was made of thick, turgid stuff. It felt like breathing molasses.

We sat in the dark motel room, shades pulled, Lisa in just her jeans, me crouched beside her in less. She was riding someone else's Wi-Fi network named, of all things, Bouncy House. Her face was bathed blue in the glow of the screen.

She was a ghost.

I spoke as we scrolled through the site, my voice as hollow as my childhood. When we clicked through to new pages the language was garbled, a mishmash of some Romance tongue, but Lisa tapped the keys and it shifted into rudely translated English. She showed me that there were options for Russian and Chinese. Japanese. Farsi. No matter the tongue, the background screens were in army green. The writing militaristic in its brevity and style.

"How do you know how to do this?"

"I take classes at Bunker Hill." She read my confusion and added, "Community college. I'm not gonna be stuck in a salon forever."

She rubbed her fingertips on her jeans every few minutes. To rid herself of the greasy stink of the machine or the murderous intent of the website, I wasn't sure. Didn't care. I could smell her beneath my own sweat.

I recognized an icon and she followed my pointing finger, clicking us through to a page of videos, my private channel of murder. I tapped the file marked BONFIRE and she clicked.

A square video opened up and footage of the struggle at the bonfire unfurled, eerie in its silence. "There she is, the bitch," Lisa hissed.

"Volume," I snapped and she hit a button.

"...almost roasted by a real wild crew in Vermont," the distorted voice regaled us. "But you know how it goes, they missed and he rolled."

When the footage began to loop, I made a cutting gesture and Lisa stopped the video. I scanned the other titles, noticing THE QUIET MAN and several others I didn't recognize. MEN'S ROOM. JADE DRAGON. HOUSE.

My throat grew tight and I coughed through the blockage at the idea that there was some kind of video of the slaughter at Annabelle's house. Lisa clicked the file before I could tell her no.

My breath shot out like I'd been punched in the gut. Drops of spittle hit the screen.

The camera was still, obviously hidden in the kitchen, the footage poor but I could still remember the thick smell of the place. Thankfully I couldn't see the carnage in the kitchen itself, but I could just make out a foot in the hall, the rest of the body out of sight.

"John," she said, her voice stretched like a wire.

There I was on screen, entering the kitchen behind the questing barrel of my pistol. The onscreen me froze, looking at something on the floor, out of view of the camera.

"The bent-nose boys from the North End rolled the dice and came up craps," the weird, electronic siren crooned. "But they left a message for the Rooster and you all too—"

Lisa and I stabbed at the volume button, my finger mashing hers down. The voice was muted midsentence.

"Goddamnit."

"Shut up," Lisa snapped, cocking her head. "You know whose voice that is?"

"Who?"

Lisa replayed the footage and the voice filled the room. It was electronically modified from the voice I knew, but it was her.

"That's her, goddamnit. Ava, that fuckin' bitch!"

My heart gained weight and hardened, sliding down the inside of my ribcage to sit in my gut.

"What else is there?" I asked after a bit.

Lisa scrolled across the screen and selected GREATEST HITS. The story of my life was written in blood.

Everyone dead by my hand was listed, minus three. The methods were enumerated. Gun, knife and strangulation the most common. There were crime scene photos linked to some kills. More recent photos of the locations beside others. In some cases, the only photos of the target were grainy yearbook shots.

"How long did it take to put this together?" I said aloud, though I knew the answer. This wasn't measured in years, this was a decade or more of hunting, pulling up the secret threads of my life. Though it focused on business, my business of killing, the motivation behind this had to be personal.

Only personal wounds generated such hate.

Lisa opened KNOWN RESIDENCES and we discovered that this area was the weakest. A few of my places were listed in blue, fewer still in red. The Quiet Man was red. Grace's condo at the Boston waterfront too. The places that had been destroyed.

Lisa clicked on the UPDATES section of the menu bar.

"Did the mob do this?" I asked.

"It's not Italian. And look."

There was a bare-bones description of my recent dumpster diving exploits in New Hampshire.

"Jesus, they already got the job on the TM?"

Further down I recognized a name in one update. Italian. DeMarco.

"Translate that one," I said and my finger left a smear on the screen.

Lisa worked her magic and I was reading a reference to my job in Los Angeles. Neatnick DeMarco. INFORMATION ON HIRING PARTY AVAILABLE it read next to a PayPal icon. There was a date next to the update. Today's date. Lisa clicked through and we saw the cost.

"Five large to find out who paid for the hit?" I said but trailed off when I saw her shoulders shaking silently. Tiny streaks of wet flowing down the canyons of her face.

"There are so many," she said.

"Yeah."

I refused to look at her, unwilling to see my life through her eyes. I stood with a cracking of knees and limped to my pile of clothes to find my smokes. "They're trying to start these assholes fighting each other?"

"Maybe." Lisa puffed her cheeks out and exhaled hard. Her bangs were limp with perspiration. "What if they're trying to light a fire. I mean, you're still alive." She tapped another line with her finger and translated it. "They take your head and this information will be removed from the market. The hiring party remains a secret."

I limped over to the dresser when I couldn't find my cigs, picking up Lisa's Chesterfields. "Want one?"

"I'll share yours," she said.

I lit the coffin nail and let the smoke trickle out. "At least the next guys will be motivated." She didn't laugh but that was okay, it wasn't really funny.

"There's so many people looking for you," she said.

"Yeah, but…" I leaned over her shoulder and slipped the cigarette between her lips. "This is telling me who they are. Every fucking one of them except the asshole who put the site together."

"It's Ava's voice."

"You think she could put all this together?"

"She was smart enough to fool you."

I took my cigarette back and stared holes in the wall. Ava did fool me, all the way. The question was whether she was working for someone else or if this was her play all the way.

And why?

"What are you gonna do?" Lisa said.

"I hate Chesterfields, so I'm going to get some smokes and call Number Four. Tell him we got two points on the scoreboard."

I found a pay phone outside a 7-Eleven and called Number Four to read him the score. Then I told him how to meet me in New York.

- 1 -

TWENTY-EIGHT

"There are things one does and things one does not," the thin tailor said, patchy strands of long hair combed back over his oblong skull. "Scotch is preferred at Montana and Jibes."

The man and the place were old and, if a bit worn, the suit nonetheless constructed of the finest materials. His name was Jibes and he reminded me of plantations in the post-war South, grand even in disrepair. He was a lean and aging man with an aura of decrepit nobility. A landless baron without a family fortune, a naval captain without a ship. His business required a personal introduction. I hadn't seen him in years.

The shop was downtown on the second story of a building in the Financial District, where the roads grew narrow and ran like canyons between skyscrapers that leaned close to block out the sun. Off the beaten path for the hotshot traders and young guns, Montana and Jibes catered to old lions of industry, and if the business no longer paid what it once did, I sensed that the proprietor didn't mind.

"Rocks are acceptable," Jibes continued and his light shoes swished across the luxuriant rug toward a crystal decanter on a sidebar of maple beneath portraits of important men. They wore vests and waist chains and muttonchops, and not a man jack among them smiled.

Like so many places in New York City, the space I stood in echoed with the voices of previous lives. I wondered if Montana and Jibes had once been a club, or a speakeasy for the wealthy. The rooms were long and tall and possessed an elegant disdain for efficiency, the place a timeless pearl hidden in the folds of Wall Street. Only the windows revealed disarray as city grime outside the glass clutched with bent fingers. The honk of car horns was ever present. It was a dark place, a red space, and was designed to absorb sound. Deals had been made here. Schemes unfurled.

It was one of the many faces of my home and I felt welcome despite the years since my last visit.

"Neat," I said and the tailor nodded.

There are things one does.

"The gentleman will choose his fabric," was one of those things and I had selected wool. "Silk is not inappropriate in this weather," Jibes said. "You don't have the look for linen."

My look was shaven-headed with dark stubble filling the hollows of my cheeks. I'd lost weight while up north and suspected I looked ill.

"Wool," I said, and he nodded, adding, "The gentleman finds worsted acceptable?"

I nodded, unsure of what *worsted* meant.

"The current fashion is for shorter jackets, tightly fitted. It makes men look frivolous."

I nodded to show I understood.

"You are not to wear a frivolous suit. This is for business, yes? To make an impression? Not for standing in lines on sidewalks outside of clubs."

I thought of the bullets Lisa had bought me. A working man's bullets. The best kind for my gun.

"It's for a funeral and a celebration," I told him when I accepted a crystal tumbler of scotch. "And to remind me of who I am."

His eyes were watery but his gaze carried weight behind the rimless glasses perched on his nose. He was taking me in. Understanding me. Ten thousand dollars in cash had already been offered and accepted, his other appointments for the day canceled.

I sipped and let the warm liquid roll over my tongue. "And I need to be able to move in it."

"Remove your pants." He produced a tape measure from a desk

drawer as I sat to pull off my boots and then kicked my pants off into a puddle. He picked them up and smoothed them over the back of his own desk chair and may have paused a beat, only a beat, when I set a Sig Sauer 9mm semiauto on his green desk blotter.

"Shirt," he commanded and I peeled off my shirt, draping it more neatly than I otherwise might over my jeans. His wet gaze trailed over my bruised ribs and other contusions, reading the scars from older wounds.

It took him a minute of arthritic effort but he sank to his knees on the carpet and used a firm thumb to hold one end of the tape against my instep, sliding the other up against the inside of my leg until his hand brushed my groin. "Does the gentleman dress to the right or the left?"

"Huh?"

The door opened and another old man glided in, skin dark and gnarled as tree bark. He was short and wiry and though effeminate in his movements, I thought he might be dangerous. He held out a wooden cigar case.

"No, thanks…" I trailed off as he opened it to reveal a compact weapon with a nickel finish. The gun was nestled in purple velvet alongside two narrow magazines.

"Walther PPK/S, twenty-two caliber," the newcomer said with a mélange of accents I couldn't place. Off his nod I plucked the pistol from the velvet and inserted a magazine, racking the slide with a quiet snick as he closed the case and set it on the desk. He bent with less effort than Jibes and removed a cleaning kit from the bottom drawer of the desk. I recognized the sharp tang of gun oil.

A firm but gentle touch stilled me. "Henri will care for your sidearm," Jibes said as Henri sat at the desk and professionally broke down my pistol. "He served in the *Légion étrangère*. The French Foreign Legion."

"Algiers," Henri spoke quietly without looking up from his task. His fingers danced with the nimble dexterity of a pianist and I heard the tap of his sculpted nails against the weapon.

I sipped my scotch and tried not to point the Walther at Jibes as he shuffled around me taking measurements. "Montana?" I asked something I'd always wondered about, thinking this might be my last chance to solve one of life's minor mysteries. Henri smiled, embarrassed.

"He wanted an American name," Jibes said, and I set the scotch down on the rug to help him to his feet. He nodded thanks before glancing at the drink and I picked it up.

Henri removed each 9mm bullet from the ejected magazine and swiped the round with a jeweler's cloth before thumbing it back into the clip. He spoke in French and Jibes paused where he was sliding rolled tubes of fabric from a warren of cubbies on one wall.

"The suit must be cut to allow for Kevlar?" Jibes asked, and I wondered if he always had an accent or if Henri's had worn off on him. They worked together as if each movement were choreographed and I knew that they were more than simple business partners.

"I don't have any."

Henri fixed me with a look a teacher might aim at an inept student. An avalanche of French tumbled forth and I knew he had held rank in the Legion.

"You will have Kevlar," Jibes said, and when I opened my mouth, he held up his hand. "Henri says you have already paid for it."

I had forgotten about shoes but Jibes and Montana did not. I had forgotten underwear and undershirts but they did not. When Henri returned my weapon, he admonished me to clean it after it saw use. When lunch came, we ate small tuna salad sandwiches off a silver tray, and we smoked cigars while one or the other took fabric from the room and worked. The scotch was pleasant, and they were companionable men without much talking. When I first realized they would not leave me alone in the room, I thought they were afraid of robbery. Later I had the sense that they felt responsible for me and were on guard for my benefit.

The afternoon was as pleasant as the scotch, and Henri, sipping with me, spoke of far-off places. He bore a smear of scar tissue on one cheekbone and his knuckles wore the marks of brawls in foreign alleyways. We sat together swapping stories and it occurred to me that if I grew to reach old age, I'd like to carry myself the way Henri did. We talked about bullets and pistols and he removed several from a safe in the wall so we could compare them. I think he meant to include them with my suit, but I told him I was well armed. He patted my knee and told me I was a good boy.

Fine scotch indeed.

The sun was reduced to glowing coals outside the filthy window when Jibes returned with my suit on several different hangers. Henri lifted a trashcan and I peeled off my shorts, dropping them inside while Jibes unwrapped crackling cellophane and gave me a fresh set of plaid boxers, complete with creases.

I slid my feet into calf-length socks of dark grey and then stepped into trousers of charcoal, the fabric lighter and smoother than I thought wool could be. The shirt was white and Jibes helped with the cufflinks, simple silver devices that I fumbled with until he brushed my hands aside and fixed them.

The tie alone bore color, a burgundy so rich that I could see layer after layer, level after level like a building that was beautiful above the surface, but wouldn't really yield its treasures until you dug beneath the earth.

The jacket had a slight width in the middle and across my back to accommodate a protective vest, but flowed like no wool I've ever worn. The interior was silk with a silver sheen and slid like mist when I moved.

Jibes tsked and made his uncomfortable way to the floor again with a needle and thread in his teeth. He fumbled with the pant cuffs as Henri circled me, nodding.

- 2 -

The two gentlemen were backlit in the doorway to their shop, the stairs leading up to their office visible behind them. It was quiet on the sidewalk, the honk of horns mild now that the day trading was long since done. In my suit I felt like I wore the night on my shoulders and said this thing to the tailors Montana and Jibes.

In my left fist I held a heavy paper bag by the handles. Inside were additional underclothes and a six-pound bullet-resistant vest from a company called SureFire. Hidden beneath my jacket I wore a Bianchi quick draw shoulder holster for the Sig Sauer. A nylon holster held the Walther against my ankle. Gifts from Montana & Jibes.

I shook hands and turned to leave as Henri entered the building. The sound of Jibes clearing his throat was faint, surely too quiet to be heard over the background noise of the city, but I turned back.

"Yes?" I said.

"There are things one does." A streetlight flashed off of his glasses and he stood very tall. "Do them well."

TWENTY-NINE

- 1 -

I trotted up the damp stairs from the Four train platform into the underground scrum of Union Square Station, moving around a crowd surrounding three young men dancing to the beat of a single drummer and generally fucking up the flow of foot traffic. I smelled sweat, perfume and the sickly-sweet smoke of ganja.

I hipped my way through a turnstile, lifting the Montana & Jibes bag up high and ascending another wide staircase that spat me into the summer night and the outdoor party of Union Square with its trees and open spaces and surrounding restaurants and department stores. Barks and growls rose from the nearby dog park and laughter threaded through the noise. Another drummer worked a set of upended paint buckets and laid down the beat of the city. I found myself adjusting my step in response and wondered if the musician understood his power. A cluster of Hare Krishna's were chanting near a fountain, promising hope to street kids while students in blue vests offered passersby a chance to save the world.

I passed through a cluster of old black and Hispanic men with chessboards waiting on makeshift tables.

"Yo flash, try a game!"

I laughed and shook my head at the guy. Looked like a day laborer but probably played like Bobby Fischer. Students from New York

University were protesting something with a long banner they had tangled into unreadability and everywhere people sat and smoked and talked. I picked my way between them until I reached the busy crossing at Fourteenth Street.

A long yellow school bus was pulled over with its safety lights flashing to disgorge an army of kids toting band instruments. When a taxi tried to sneak around the bus, a waiting patrol car flashed blue lights and booped its siren. It snugged in tight behind the cab and an irritated voice asked over the cruiser's loudspeaker, "What are you, stupid?"

The waiting crowd around me laughed and I enjoyed the moment back home in my city, inhaling the smoke from a kebab grill and drinking in the sights and sounds of so many people speaking so many languages.

Hell, even the garbage strike had ended while I was out of town and the streets were back to normal levels of trash.

Home. Never much of a word for me, but it had taken on new meaning after the debacle in New England. I visited a wine store with a lit sign stating USQ WINES and carried my bottles and the Montana & Jibes bag into Best Buy. When I rode the escalator down with my purchases, the security guard bowed to the power of my suit and didn't ask to check any receipts. I imagined myself as an Upper East Side wife, the kind of lady who shops for sport and thinks sitting on a museum board is work. I was still chuckling and wondering if I had the energy to buy a disposable razor at the CVS across the street when I heard a voice say, "See you got a tactical vest in the bag."

I kept up my smile and turned to look into the sharp eyes of a cop.

- 2 -

Foot traffic moved all around us as we stood in the smoky lee of a Halal cart.

"Army?"

"Diplomatic security," I lied.

"They pay good?"

"Eh," I shrugged and sipped from the Coke he'd bought me, the cop.

"Man, you know what they pay us in New York?" He spoke around his hotdog, and I nodded like I knew what a New York City police officer earned per annum. He was built square without much neck, flame tattoos visible beneath the short sleeves of his black uniform shirt. He paused when the radio in his car squawked and said something into the mic clipped to his shoulder then continued with me. "But private pays good, right?"

"Contracting pays great," I thumped my chest to release a quiet burp. A bicycle whizzed past close enough to touch and a truck grinding through traffic blatted its horn. Girls passing by drowned out everything with their laughter.

"That suit…" He raked his eyes up and down my body like I was a supermodel and I gave him a chuckle.

"Client bought it."

"Shit."

"Gotta look right, places he goes."

"You going to Lincoln Center and stuff?"

"Like that."

"You get to travel much?"

"I work in the States. Some guys work overseas but the rules are different."

He nodded like he understood and crumpled his napkin, tossing it in a nice arc into a trashcan from fifteen feet away.

"Three points," he grinned. "Your company ever hire cops?"

I nodded. "Cops and military, mostly. If you have executive protection experience then they really want you."

"I did the mayor's detail."

"Tell them that." I pretended to look in my wallet for a card and shook my head at him. "Shit, I don't have a card. You?"

"Sure," he pulled out his wallet, a fat leather monstrosity stuffed with slips of paper. He slid out a bent card and handed it over.

"I'll email you with a link so you can check the company out. Hit me back when you're ready so I can knock on the door."

"Hey, thanks man." His radio squawked again and he cursed. "I caught a call."

"No worries," I replied. "Hey, you know a place called Lips?" I picked up my bag as he laughed.

"The drag queen joint?"

"Job takes me to interesting places."

He pointed west down Fourteenth Street. "Straight down there until you hit Seventh Avenue and cut south. It's on Christopher."

Then he was in his car and pulling out into traffic with a flash of his roof lights to clear a path. He triggered his siren once and I waved.

- 3 -

Part of the plan had come to me back in New Hampshire, but my mind had been muddled from Wade's chemical party and I needed to get home by myself. See if the energy flowing up through the sidewalks would power me the way that only New York can.

I also wanted to see if they'd kill me as soon as I hit the city limits. Lisa was made out of the same material as Sean and wanted to come with me. A girl who'd never even been to New York but ready to deal herself in all the way.

I did the only thing I could to honor Sean's memory after all his family had sacrificed. I sent her home.

It was on Third Avenue outside a Meatheads taco joint when I found a working pay phone. I ignored the stickiness on the receiver as barhoppers wandered past in loud groups.

In the end it turned out there was one more thing I could do for Lisa and hung up the phone without calling.

THIRTY

"Whiskey, anything American, neat."

"Oh c'mon, live a little." Her voice was an advertisement to visit Queens and scratchy from cigarettes.

"I like whiskey."

"Doll, ask for a whiskey sour and I'll make it a double."

I grinned even though it hurt my face, and nodded. She sauntered back to the bar, weaving through the round cocktail tables with sauce in her hips, and I wasn't the only one watching.

A fan dancer was working the stage while a tall beauty in purple satin belted Linda Ronstadt into a standing microphone. A deeper voice than you'd expect if you didn't know where you were.

It was dark but lively, the mood full of sass and electricity. The surroundings were velvet and satin, tasseled lamps were atop the tables lining the walls. The middle tables where the crowds gathered were a lampless forest of balloon glasses and tall-stemmed martini types glowing with an alchemy of liquids. It was the kind of place that would look good even in daylight.

Holiday Lounge it was not.

But it was alive in a way that I admired, and if I expected to live, I'd have planned on coming back. I saw guys that looked gay and girls that might be, a couple of old queens at the bar were what you'd expect.

But there were three tables full of people in business clothes, clearly on an after-work binge, and a heavyset man and woman who did not dress New York were singing along, the man with even more gusto than his wife.

Funny what you notice when the lights are going out.

My ankle sent me a few irritated calls that I ignored and my ribs set to ringing on another line. I was about to pull out my bottle of Children's Tylenol when she came back. A squat pillar of a glass balanced on her tray, simpler than the cocktail glasses on other tables. She set it down with perfect aim and without spilling a drop, dead center on a black coaster that was new and nearly invisible against the black tabletop. The drink was a hundred shades of chocolate beneath the tasseled lamp.

"My name's Selene," she said and winked. "Pull my leash when you want me."

I felt like I should say something so I went with, "My glass is simpler than those." I touched the garnish of a maraschino cherry and nudged the lemon rind until the ice clinked.

She cocked a hip and posed with a tray in a way that should look phony but didn't and came back with, "Right glass for the right drink."

"There are things one does," I said quietly.

"What, baby?"

She toed out the chair opposite mine without keeling over in her heels and slid into the seat.

I sipped my drink—smooth—and said, "Thing a friend of mine said. 'There are things one does.'"

She planted an elbow on the table and rested her chin in her hand, eyeing the bandage on my face. "Hey, you need a rescue?"

I choked back a laugh and sipped to cover it. Fuck, this drink was smooth. "You gonna get in trouble?"

She flexed her free hand like her fingers were tipped with razors instead of long red nails and said, "I am trouble."

So I picked her for my play. I told myself that, though to be honest, maybe I just wanted to share the last good time. I told her about the Holiday Lounge where I normally drank cheap whiskey and about a bad trip up to New England. The funerals of some friends was how I spun it. I sipped. And felt the cocktail loosening me up and told her how good it felt to be home.

"And you picked here?" she said.

"Yeah."

"Been here before?"

"Once on a business thing, like those guys." I pointed at the office crowd across the floor. Unlike them, I'd killed the guy I left with.

Onstage the fan dancer worked her deceptions, never letting you see what you thought you were going to see. I pulled out my little white bottle and Selene shook her head. "Management's tough about that stuff. Use the men's room."

"This? Ranger candy."

"Who or what is Ranger candy?"

I showed her the label and smiled when she said, "Children's Tylenol?"

I shook the bottle and two pills tumbled onto my tongue. "Rangers use it to dull pain on long marches."

"You're in the Army?"

I shook my head. "Just a thing I read."

The music changed, a piano and stand-up bass behind a singer crooning about not going home with any guy that didn't have an air conditioner. Selene's eyes grew wider while I spoke, as if I were telling her some kind of fish story. When I sucked on the ice before crunching it, she reached out and dragged her nails lightly across my wrist.

"My god, baby, you're straight? Like really straight?"

"Well, yeah."

She leaned back and laughed. "You are too good to be true." And slid out of the seat, making my glass vanish like a stage magician. She produced a little RESERVED sign from somewhere and slid it onto her side of the table, nudging the seat back in with her hip. "This'll protect you," and she was gone, slithering and slinking back through the tables, pausing to take an order here and there, touching shoulders a lot.

I got my drink first, which was something, but Selene didn't sit down again, which was also something. Probably for the best, though. I was getting a little too easy and didn't need to get smashed. And it was time to do what I'd come to do.

I slipped Wade's laptop from the sleek briefcase I'd bought and kickstarted it, flipping through pages until it landed on Recent Updates. A little typing with both of my index fingers and then I stood, leaving the machine partially closed on my seat. The tip I trapped beneath my drink because it would help my message find its way to the target.

I waited until it got loud onstage, three ladies in slinky black on three microphones, and ghosted my way around the edge of the club until I could slip past the doorman, a guy my height with twice my mass, most of it in his shoulders.

That tip? Pair of one-hundred-dollar bills. Selene was one of the good ones and helped make the last good time even better.

Excited voices were raised in conversation as a quartet of men passed by on the sidewalk, moving around me as if I were a rock in a stream. Up and down the street the restaurants had their big windows and sliding walls open in summery invitation. The air was thick with incoming weather, and over the whoosh of traffic and honking horns I heard the sky growl with warning thunder. Maybe meant for me.

I smoothed my jacket and felt the pistol in its holster. A scuff of my foot told me the ankle holster was in place. Red business lay ahead.

"Hey!"

I turned as Selene pushed herself past the doorman, looking as out of place on the sidewalk as a white tiger roaming Central Park.

"You can't leave this much," she said, holding up the two bills. The doorman noticed and shook his head.

"I can and I did." I found my cigarettes and pulled out the pack.

"What the fuck?" If she was glamorous, it was a New York kind of glamour.

"I needed a boost and you gave me that," I said, wanting to be gone.

"Hey," she said, and those long nails grazed my injured cheek with the delicacy of a feather. "You look terrible, honey. Why so sad?"

I hadn't realized how much sorrow was riding my bloodstream until she pointed an arrow at it, but the weight of it wanted to drag me to the pavement.

She saw everything I might say reflected in my eyes. Her finger-nails stayed on my cheek for a moment and I watched her shoulders sag beneath the weight she was trying to draw from me.

When she went back inside the club it was without a word.

I lit my cigarette and tossed the match into the gutter, watching the glowing arc like one of Wade's crazy catapults.

"Hey," I said the doorman. "What time is it?"

"It's 1:30 a.m."

It began to rain.

THIRTY-ONE

- 1 -

My new shoes swished down the blue patterned hall carpeting as I moved quickly but quietly past tall doors of dark brown oak. Everything in the Waldorf Astoria spoke of old New York elegance and chief among the offered amenities was the quiet oasis the hotel created in the middle of the city.

I'd splurged for a night.

My suit jacket was heavy with damp from the storm and even the Waldorf Astoria couldn't blunt the sound of angry weather outside. Water trickled in streams from my scalp, but even so I could feel the prickle of sweat at my temples, the water springing up from inside me so much heavier with poison and pain than the cleansing rain.

Asked to name the emotion that gripped my heart, I wouldn't have been able. But I could describe it. The sloshing weight in my gut. The urge to turn away. To close my eyes against what I knew.

Quickened breath whistled over my teeth between parted lips.

Enough.

The magnetic door locks were a necessary anachronism, and I paused as if to fiddle with my tie while glancing up and down the hallway for an unwanted audience.

My left hand dipped into a pocket and cupped the closed straight razor, a recent purchase, in my palm. I swiped my magnetic card across the sensor and stuck it in my teeth before drawing the Sig Sauer from the shoulder holster, the move choreographed a hundred times during my quiet march up the hall.

The tiny LED light blinked green, and as soon as I heard the muffled thump of the mechanism disengaging, I hit it with my shoulder and flowed inside, pistol tracking.

I was alone.

Rain beat a tattoo against windows framed in heavy blue drapes, and the polished wooden furniture of the sitting room glowed bronze in the lowered lighting.

The carpet was a deep burgundy here but no less forgiving of noise, and I moved silently toward the open double doors leading into the bedroom.

My eyes were adjusting to the dim space, but my first instinct had been correct. Nothing was amiss in the bedroom. The elegant king-sized bed had been turned down but not slept in. Red numbers from a nightstand clock glowed.

I heard the hissing of water from the bathroom.

Unsure about the old building's ability to absorb the sharp report of a firearm, I would use the blade if I could.

I ghosted to the partially closed door, gliding to my right away from the spill of light, the movement taking my gun offline so I slid on the oblique, a fencer's stance with the 9mm aimed forward, shoulder blades aimed at the wall behind me. I felt the dresser against my hip and used it as a guide to approach the bathroom.

The smell of steam and shampoo.

I crouched low and swiveled into the bathroom, shouldering the door open wider as whorls of steam screamed false movement cues and urged me to fire-fire-fire.

On the fogged mirror over the brass fixtures of the sink she had taped a note. Steam had loosened the glue and it hung by an edge. Another hour and it would have fallen to the veined marble floor.

I could feel the painful dig of the razor in my clenching left fist as I nudged the flap of the note up with the barrel of my pistol.

I'M SORRY,
AVA

"You fucking bitch," I snarled, bluffing against an invisible, crashing blow to my solar plexus. Hollow winds roared through my emptied rib cage and my stomach churned with the certitude of what I had known. It's one thing to understand mentally that you fell for a woman who wants you dead. It's another thing to understand it in the gut.

I understood.

She had set the dogs on me.

Ava.

- 2 -

I smoked for a while and sipped scotch in a cut crystal glass from the sitting room's sideboard. My damp suit clung to me, drying in the cold air blowing from a hidden vent high in the wall. I could take it off. Let it dry.

Instead, I stayed seated and shivered.

I told myself I was waiting for the vicious rain outside to let up, a jilted lover of a storm if ever there was one.

But the Sig stayed on my knee as I drank with my left hand, unaware of how comfortable the baroque wingback chair was, fantasizing about the click of the lock and her dark silhouette in the doorway. She knew where I was and hadn't brought the army. Had come to the Waldorf herself.

Why?

Sipping, clumsy, clinking the glass against my teeth and coughing against the smooth liquid designed for a palate more refined than my own.

This way was madness.

She wanted me to dance at the end of her strings.

Wanted me dead.

After another drink, I realized I knew who she really was.

THIRTY-TWO

- 1 -

North Brother Island was a hump of inky black in the darkness of the East River. Across the way, the towers of Manhattan glowed as if they were made of jewels, and the great bridges that spanned the river were shining arches shimmering in the rain.

Thirty-three acres of ruins and overgrowth, an apocalyptic jungle within swimming distance of Manhattan. Swimming distance if the current didn't drown you first and spit your bloated corpse into the sea lanes. Propeller bait for the great tankers and cargo ships that fed the biggest city in the country.

North Brother Island, site of New York City's largest disaster until 9/11, the foundering of the steamboat General Slocum which spilled its human cargo into the foaming wash.

North Brother Island, the ruins of the quarantine hospital which played host to countless coughing deaths, tucked safely away from the glittering carriages and living theater of the city.

No one visited the island anymore. No one was allowed. The wooden waterfront had largely collapsed and rotted away. The red brick hospital and barracks buildings, long since abandoned, had fallen or stood according to an arcane agreement with the flora that consumed them, stems splitting brick walls and roots buckling floors.

It was a place of moss and rubble. Of scuttling rats and screeching birds. Ancient smoke stacks towered above the trees and tuberculosis wards huddled in the undergrowth.

North Brother Island.

My invitation to Chin said festivities would begin at 5:00 p.m. I suspected he would be early. You know, that kind of guest.

But he was careful. Strategic. His attack would be devastating, but I planned to be ready.

So Number Four dropped me off in his Gloucester fishing boat well before dawn. We ran without lights, hidden by sheets of rain.

"You tell Lisa?" I shouted over the weather.

"No way. She's royally pissed!"

The river danced under the watery bombardment as Number Four nosed the rocking boat near enough to shore that I could flounder against the current towing an inflatable raft containing my party favors. He pushed off a flotilla of rubber tires, formerly dock bumpers, carrying bladders of gasoline.

I was exhausted by the time it was all on shore, the tires proving difficult to drag up against the current. But rubber burns with the kind of greasy fire that would serve me well even during the storm and I fought to bring them all to land.

The current sucked my raft away when it was empty and I thought about Cortez burning his ships at the shoreline so his men would know there was no retreat.

When I had my breath back, I called to mind the maps I'd studied and grabbed as much as I could carry in a single load.

There wasn't much time.

I worked quickly through the dark I had left to me, depleting my store of weapons more rapidly than expected as I built several caches of guns leading back toward a small pile of explosives in the brick-walled, semi-intact main hospital building. My own personal Alamo.

"Cortez was a bitch," I said to the jungle but heard no reply.

The storm drove me with its urgent beat, thunder crashing overhead like a gong that shivered the air while the rain beat down like Japanese taiko drums. I wished I had a giant fucking sound system and "White Rabbit" playing on an endless loop.

Grace was right, I did prefer to work up close. Fire and smoke would bring me together with my enemies and I set most of my flammables in the Alamo, creeping over moss-slick piles of rubble and past cave-ins, making small stacks of tires and fuel. I splashed some of the liquid around where it wouldn't be washed away by leaking rainfall.

I wished I was Wade. I wished I had time to build a Ouija board and summon his crazy ghost to help me construct my trap.

Exhausted and wearing only shorts, skin welted from whipping branches and torn from falls among the rocks, I found a nest with my penlight and settled myself into the corner of an old brick house with enough roof to make it popular among the vermin set. The rats were bold but sensed something unnatural and surrendered the space to me.

I chewed up a protein bar and drank a bottle of water. Pissed to mark the place as mine.

My entire body was a screaming ache, and I disputed not a single mosquito when it drank from me while I pulled dry clothes from a waterproof bag and put them on over sweat-sticky skin. Blue cargo pants from Old Navy—they didn't have black in my size—the pockets good for holding extra magazines. A black T-shirt over which I slung a fishing vest, modified to hold more ammunition and two fragmentation grenades.

Oh, those gun-happy Townie Mafia boys.

I hung two surplus Marine Ka-Bar fighting knives from my belt. The razor was in my pocket. The 9mm Sig beneath my armpit in the shoulder holster. Henri's .380 gift still adorned my ankle. I stuck a few more surprises in available pockets and settled a Yankees cap on my head.

With an M-16 rifle cradled in my arms I let iron weights drag down my eyelids. Rat claws ticked against nearby bricks and the rain made a curtain of sound around me.

There was more to do. Pits to be dug. Trip wires to be strung. But it would wait until morning. Had to wait. I had no energy left.

I slept like every sentry in the world.

- 2 -

"I am like one segment of an endless invisible worm. Unkillable. Eternal. But the slope to reincarnation is steep and slow to climb."

My eyelids scraped up over dried eyeballs as the words echoed in my mind. Fucking hell, I'd rather wake up to screams than the bubbling ugliness kicked up by my id. It was the reason I made it a strict policy to avoid dreams and hallucinogens.

Why was I awake?

I straightened my crooked cap and tried to listen past the drumming rain, flexing my left leg, pants soaked from a leak in the ceiling.

Something swept by overhead. Movement?

A flashlight beam. It passed by again, the circle of illumination flickering and dancing as it stabbed through gaps behind me to play over the wall opposite.

My hands took up the rifle with great care and I eased the selector switch to three-round burst. It was hard to hear over the rain and I stood, picking my way by feel over the uneven floor. A twisted ankle now might as well be a death sentence.

Easing a metal gas can onto its side I unscrewed the cap, wincing at the loud glug of fuel as it spilled over the ground, my eyes watering from the fumes. I lit a cigarette and balanced it where the slightest brush would knock it off.

Fuck fuck fuck.

I put a burner phone down beside the smoldering cigarette and took the other with me, pausing to memorize the number of the first. My plan coming together on the fly.

Voices now. More than one. Russian.

At the open door I lowered myself quietly, aware of the clink and rattle of the magazines in my pockets. The rain hadn't let up at all. When we killers met it would be an intimate affair, blind and deaf as we stumbled together.

I chanced it and quick-stepped from the opening to a nearby wall and scuttled into cover, suppressing a curse as a magazine tumbled from a thigh pocket. I was bending to pick it up when I saw the orange glow of a cigarette floating toward me around the side of the building.

Stupid but maybe not unexpected. Chin had moved fast to seize the initiative, faster than I had planned. He'd activated whatever troops were ready to rock and roll right away, and the Russians were always ready for blood.

Clumsy though.

Two more men followed the third, faces a pale blur, street clothes soaked, the point man picking his way with a penlight mounted on some kind of submachine gun.

It took an effort of will to tear my eyes from them but I checked out my phone and made sure the volume button on the side was off before dialing.

The beautiful music of a ring tone drifted from the old house, barely audible over the storm.

"Tikho." The point man held up a fist like he'd seen on TV and the group halted before changing direction toward the house. I ended my call.

A laughing god of cruel disposition smiled down at North Brother Island. Less than a minute after the last man went inside voices were raised in fear when orange light bloomed from the open door and windows.

I rested the M-16 on the wall and drew a bead on the doorway, waiting for a shadow to block the flames.

A gentle squeeze.

Two feet of fire stabbed out and the gun bucked off the wall, but the lead Russian fell back inside. I fired two more bursts into the doorway and could hear them screaming then, trapped between the gasoline blaze and my bullets. Already the stink of burning meat rode the night and it wasn't a minute before one of them tried to scramble out of a window, pant cuffs dripping flames.

I put two bursts into him and ejected the spent magazine, reloading a full one with a slap against the bottom to seat it.

First blood was mine.

- 3 -

Death danced on an island of fire and smoke.

It was blinding. Maddening. The sharp crack of gunfire rising over the slam of the deluge. Twice I ran into groups and dove away into the brush to leave a grenade in my wake. I fought the red urge to finish the wounded and left them screaming, adding spice to my stew of confusion.

The fires I'd prepared were slowly destroying the ruined buildings despite the rain, whipped into frenzy by hot flares and gasoline. The black smoke was pressed down by the storm as it tried to strangle the conflagration and conjured a more hellish environment than I'd hoped to create.

I lost my rifle after the second grenade but stumbled into one of my caches, left earlier beneath a spiral staircase in a separate hospital building. They found me squatting there, reloading my pockets with ammunition, easy prey if they had paused and had the patience to aim. But they were panicked men, outside their element in war and charging behind their barking pistols. I'd left an AK-47 locked and loaded at the cache and the thunder of 7.62 rounds on full automatic filled the hospital wing, bright flashes lighting the room in kaleido-scopic flares that left me disoriented and blind.

Someone crashed into me and we rolled across the ground, grunt-ing and punching. I felt up along one of his thighs and jerked a knee up hard, bucking him off me. Slithering on him in a motion as sexual as it was violent, I gutted him with a Ka-Bar, leaving it in him as he jerked and gurgled.

Breathing was difficult and I wrapped a kerchief around the lower half of my face. I listened for sirens but could hear nothing. The police and fire departments must be going mad as the unused island erupted in battle.

AK in one hand, a satchel in the other, I slipped outside and coughed again from the smoke.

It would be worse for them.

The crack and rattle of gunfire sounded from near and far on the thirty-three-acre island, the frightened attackers firing at shadows. My eyes watered and my balls contracted in animal reaction as the beast within counted the number of my enemy. But a sound pealed forth. My sound. The howl of the yellow dog.

It was time for the Alamo and the final fight. By whatever fucked-up god was watching this mess, I'd give them everything I had.

A long flame stabbed out from the night and a mule kicked me in the head.

- 4 -

I came to consciousness aware of a searing line of pain over my left ear. I was already crawling, dragging my satchel, the assault rifle lost.

Bullets *spanged* off the wall behind me and chips of red brick bounced off the back of my protective vest. Reconnaissance by fire, they weren't sure where I was. I heard Spanish and wondered what kind of motley assembly had come to kill me. Chin had sacrificed quality for speed in assembling his force. Maybe they'd start shooting each other.

Blood and smoke. I couldn't see anything but guessed at the direction of their shots and pulled a very special item from my satchel. It was faintly curved, the size of a hardcover book.

FRONT TOWARD ENEMY read the raised lettering on one curved side, and I wriggled forward as far as I dared before stabbing the two prongs at its base into the soggy ground.

I scrambled back trailing a wire as more bullets screamed through the night and my back met the hard wall too soon. I squatted, a whimpering goblin dripping bloody snot, and clacked the control in my fist.

It was a noise so tremendous that time slowed and the night paused to nod in recognition at such mighty carnage.

The Claymore mine detonated a shaped charge, hurling hundreds of steel ball bearings toward the enemy, the canister shot of the modern age. Unholy terror on unprotected infantry.

The concussion made me convulse and pressure slammed against my eardrums as the night and smoke were swept aside by the incredible power of the weapon. For a split second I saw half a dozen frozen ghosts looking in my direction. In the next moment they were gone. Vanished. Wet shreds of them scattered.

A tree toppled with a tremendous crash, the sound muffled. I shook my head and tried to unscramble my senses.

Move move move.

- 5 -

While trying to locate the cache I'd hidden in an old church, I'd become disoriented and found myself at the edge of the water while shots tore the night asunder behind me. "Fuck."

Spotlights stabbed out from the river and an amplified voice commanded, "CEASE FIRE!"

It had all the effect you might expect.

There were at least three patrol boats out there. I wasn't sure if they were NYPD or Coast Guard and didn't want to find out.

I was creeping back into the lee of a tree when a group moved by, four of them bent double and trotting in a line. They wore hoodies and jeans but moved like they had training, each one carrying a pistol. Whoever they were, this unit was more skilled or smarter than the rest of the horde and had read this bad deal for what it was.

I slipped in behind them after drawing Henri's .380 from the holster at my ankle, my plan uncertain but my appetite for blood not yet satiated.

A sleek, metal boat was pulled up in the rocky surf far from the docks, tied to something I couldn't see. The quartet made their way toward it and I broke from the trees behind them, stepping lightly until I caught up with the last man in line. The first two men had already waded into the river, their guns held up high over the water.

From two feet away I planted my feet and pulled the trigger, putting a high velocity slug through the back of his hood. He went down like I'd hit him with an axe.

The second man was still turning in confusion when I fired twice and he jerked once, stumbling. I took a careful, sideways stance, my arm at full extension before firing at his center mass.

He sat down hard before slowly toppling to the side.

I dove to my belly as rounds cracked over my head, one of the hooded men firing wildly at what must have been to him only indiscernible movement in the dark. His muzzle flash marked him, and I braced my elbows in the mud before squeezing the trigger.

The last man from the crew was wading back through the churning water and trying to take aim, buffeted by the stormy toss.

I waited for his approach, discerning the white of his eyes but no detail of his face, wondering who he was and then smashing his identity from him with my final bullet.

I slid the empty pistol back into the ankle holster and drew the strap across it to secure the weapon. Smoke billowed from the trees behind me as the storm strangled the fires and the gunshots had grown sporadic. Whether the men were regaining discipline or there simply weren't many of them left, I didn't know and didn't care.

I had a boat to steal.

- 6 -

I never heard the shot.

I was knee-deep in the river trying to steal the boat when something punched me hard between the shoulder blades and I tripped face forward into the craft, stunned and unmoving.

A man landed on me, his slashing arc of steel separating the tie line as he scrambled over me like a dead thing and engaged the small motor at the rear of the raft.

Sonofabitch must have followed me while I was following the hoodie crew.

We banged off the rocks before he got the metal boat turned and then we were spitting out into the river.

He saw my eyes were open and I saw his widen in recognition.

The moment stretched.

He lunged like a cobra and I felt his blade score across the front of my Kevlar vest before tearing a sharp line across my shoulder. I screamed, catching his wrist in one hand before his elbow clipped my wounded temple and I sagged, twisting an uppercut into his groin only to have my fist glance across his thigh.

He had to be one of Chin's own men, sent to ride herd on the motley assembly of thugs the crime lord had hurled at me. He was strong and scared and trained and would have killed me immediately if not for the crazy movement of the boat.

I rose to my knees and dragged out my remaining Ka-Bar, but

his knuckles connected with the inside of my elbow and my forearm turned to ice. I didn't see the next blow but found myself on my back against the thrumming bottom of the raft as he scrambled atop me and lifted his own knife overhead.

The spotlight was bright enough to carry force and a hot wind of radiance fixed our small craft in its furious glare.

He was quick, my killer, and immediately rolled over the port gunwale of the raft.

I pulled together every ounce of strength I had left and rolled over the starboard side to let the current take me.

THIRTY-THREE

The Holiday Lounge was dark and stank of smoke from cheap cigarettes. I shivered against the cold leaking in through the flimsy door. In this joint the way you warmed up was by drinking something brown from a glass. The shiver was an involuntary tick from my time in the river. I was always cold these days. Always trying to breathe.

I slipped my coins into the cigarette machine in back and pulled the knob to free a pack of Viceroys.

"Oh, fuck you."

I jiggled the knob and banged the heels of both hands against the machine, earning a, "Hey!" from the lady behind the bar but no Viceroys.

"This thing ate my money."

"What'd you want?" she asked, north of fifty and looking it, a faded rose tattooed into the wrinkled skin of her neck. An old man with lank, yellow hair tickling his collar turned his head on a rusty swivel to watch the byplay, and the box TV mounted in the corner showed a couple of heavyset women fighting in front of a cheering crowd while a commentator pretended concern.

"Viceroys," I said.

"Smoke a fuckin' man's cigarette," she said and slapped a handful of silver on the bar. The old rummy was muttering, "Man's cigarette, man's cigarette," as I scooped up the change when he changed to, "Hey, pal…"

I gave him the shoulder and limped back to the machine to get a pack of Lucky Strikes. Another whiskey or two and the pain would leave the leg along with the limp. I got my cancer sticks, turned around and stopped.

Ava was sitting on the stool next to mine and the bartender—Kathy, I think—smiled like she knew her. "What'll you have?"

I'd been going to the Holiday for years and all I ever got was a grunt.

Ava looked good, her hair longer. She had on jeans and a sweater against the autumn chill and wore them like they were an evening gown.

I sat down on my stool and she said, "You've lost weight."

I grunted. Thought about the .380 strapped to my ankle. Sipped my drink and tapped the glass once to get Kathy's attention.

"I've been coming around here, looking for you."

I didn't say anything. I hadn't been in for a while. Too busy hiding and healing.

"I haven't told anyone else about this place," she said.

I lipped a cigarette from the pack and crumpled the cellophane in my fist. Felt the pop of my knuckles before I saw she had a lighter out and a flame grew from the tip.

The matches were in my left pocket, the side away from her, so I turned that way and lit myself as Kathy set my drink down and sloshed half of it on the scratched bar.

Ava let her flame go out.

"Você matou meu pai." Ava tapped her own cigarette loose from my pack and lit it. Sucked in smoke and let it roll back out of her mouth in a cloud. *"Eu sou filha do meu pai.* That's Portuguese. You killed my father," Ava looked into the mirror and our eyes met in the glass. "I am my father's daughter." She tapped ash into a metal ashtray without looking away from my eyes in the mirror. "I was seventeen when the curses were tattooed beneath my breasts. The bruja told me the curse wouldn't work until I was developed. Until my mother's milk could be turned to poison."

She sipped and the pink tip of her tongue licked moisture from her lips.

"The same age as you when you shot my father."

Kathy caught the ugly undercurrent and urged the old man down the bar away from us, luring him with a can of Budweiser.

"Why'd you do it?" Ava asked and I was glad for the mirror. I think if I'd met her stare head on it would have boiled the liquid in my eyes.

"Impress a girl," I said.

"You did."

We smoked in silence and drank for a bit. "Why..." I stared but there were too many questions and I stalled out, so she picked one.

"You weren't who you were supposed to be and I'd become someone I didn't want to be. By the time I found out it was too late and the play was the play."

I turned on my stool and faced her. She favored me with a glance. "I..." I trailed off again. Shook my head.

"I'm glad you didn't die on that island," she said. "Twenty-three people did, but not the Rooster. Not the Rooster."

"Ava, I—" She cut me off with the tips of her fingers against my lips. She leaned in and kissed me, saying, "Don't. I need to hate you."

She moved without hurrying and left me at the bar. I like to imagine she hesitated before pushing through the door, but I couldn't afford to pretend. I'm in the business of hard truths. The hardest.

Her cigarette had smoldered to grey powder in the ashtray before I stood and slung on my denim jacket.

I already knew how many people died on North Brother Island and had done the math. I'd factored in the two dead in New Hampshire.

Spread across the country were a hundred and eighty people drinking and fucking and smoking right now. They were walking around at the very moment Ava left me at the Holiday Lounge. No idea I was coming.

I dropped a crumpled handful of bills on the bar. "Time to settle up," I said. Kathy scooped up my money so fast I expected her nails to carve up curls of wood. She didn't offer change.

Chicago first, then Los Angeles. Dallas next if I was still alive.

It was time to settle up.

THE END

ABOUT THE AUTHOR

John C. Foster was born in Sleepy Hollow, New York, and has been afraid of the dark for as long as he can remember. A writer of thrillers and dark fiction, Foster was raised in the wilds of southern New Hampshire before hauling stakes for the ersatz glow of Los Angeles. He has since relocated to the relative sanity of NYC.

Foster is an enthusiastic amateur cook, partially to offset all the griping that results from pushing his increasingly decrepit body through the rigors of martial arts training.

John's first novel, *Dead Men,* was published by Perpetual Motion Machine Publishing (PMMP) in 2015 and his second novel, *Mister White,* was published by Grey Matter Press in April of 2016. His debut collection of short stories, *Baby Powder and Other Terrifying Substances*, and the the novel *Night Roads* were published by PMMP in 2017. In 2018, GMP published his New England gothic thriller *The Isle*.

His short stories have appeared in numerous magazines and anthologies including *Shock Totem, Dark Moon Digest* and Dread – *The Best of Grey Matter Press* among others.

He lives in Brooklyn with the actress Linda Jones and their dog Coraline.

MORE DARK FICTION FROM
GREY MATTER PRESS

––––––––––

"Grey Matter Press has managed to establish itself as one of the premiere purveyors of horror fiction currently in existence via both a series of killer anthologies — *SPLATTERLANDS, OMINOUS REALITIES, EQUILIBRIUM OVERTURNED* — and John F.D. Taff's harrowing novella collection *THE END IN ALL BEGINNINGS*."

- *FANGORIA Magazine*

––––––––––

GREY MATTER
P R E S S

A DARK THRILLER

MISTER
WHITE

THE NOVEL

DO
NOT
SPEAK
HIS
NAME

JOHN C.
FOSTER

MISTER WHITE
BY JOHN C. FOSTER

In the shadowy world of international espionage and governmental black ops, when a group of American spies go bad and inadvertently unleash an ancient malevolent force that feeds on the fears of mankind, a young family finds themselves in the crosshairs of a frantic supernatural mystery of global proportions with only one man to turn to for their salvation.

Combine the intricate, plot-driven stylings of suspense masters Tom Clancy and Robert Ludlum, add a healthy dose of Clive Barker's dark and brooding occult horror themes, and you get a glimpse into the supernatural world of international espionage that the chilling new horror novel *Mister White* is about to reveal.

John C. Foster's *Mister White* is a terrifying genre-busting suspense shocker that, once and for all, answer the question you dare not ask: "Who is Mister White?"

"*Mister White* is a potent and hypnotic brew that blends horror, espionage and mystery. Foster has written the kind of book that keeps the genre fresh and alive and will make fans cheer. Books like this are the reason I love horror fiction." – Ray Garton, Grand Master of Horror and Bram Stoker Award®-nominated author of *Live Girls* and *Scissors*

"*Mister White* is like Stephen King's *The Stand* meets Ian Fleming's James Bond with Graham Masterton's *The Manitou* thrown in for good measure. It's frenetically paced, spectacularly gory and eerie as hell. Highly recommended!" – John F.D. Taff, Bram Stoker Award®-nominated author of *The End in All Beginnings*

GREY MATTER
P R E S S

greymatterpress.com

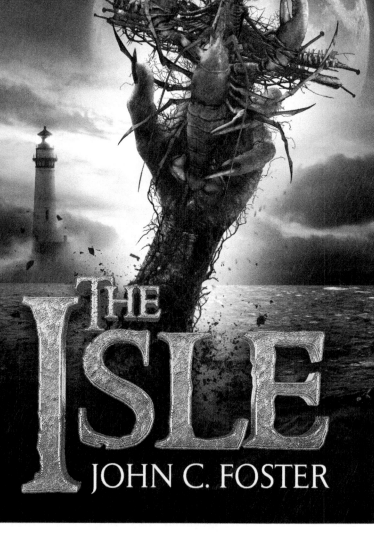

"A 21st Century contribution to the tradition of the New England Gothic from one of Nathaniel Hawthorne's fantasies."
-- John Langan, Bram Stoker Award-winning author of *The Fisherman*

THE ISLE

JOHN C. FOSTER

THE ISLE
BY JOHN C. FOSTER

A deadly menace threatens a remote island community and every man, woman and child is in peril. Sent to the isle to collect the remains of a dead fugitive, US Marshal Virgil Bone is trapped by torrential storms.

As the body count rises the community unravels, and Bone is thrust into the role of investigator. Aided by a local woman and the town pariah, he uncovers the island's macabre past and its horrifying connection to the killings.

Some curses are best believed.

Sometimes the past is best left buried.

And some will kill to keep it so.

"John Foster makes a twenty-first century contribution to the tradition of the New England Gothic, taking his lawman protagonist off the coast of the mainland United States to an island whose inhabitants might have settled there from one of Nathaniel Hawthorne's Puritan fantasies. Fast-moving, gripping, it's a tale straight from Old Man Atlantic's barnacled treasure chest." — John Langan, Bram Stoker Award-winning author of *The Fisherman*

"Brooding and claustrophobic, one hell of a scary ride. You won't soon forget your visit to *The Isle*." — Tom Deady, Bram Stoker Award-winning author of *Haven*

GREY MATTER
P R E S S

greymatterpress.com

MANIFEST
RECALL

ALAN BAXTER

"GRABS YOU BY THE NECK AND NEVER LETS GO."
— JOHN F.D. TAFF, BRAM STOKER AWARD-NOMINATED AUTHOR OF
THE END IN ALL BEGINNINGS

MANIFEST RECALL
BY ALAN BAXTER

Following a psychotic break, Eli Carver finds himself on the run, behind the wheel of a car that's not his own, and in the company of a terrified woman he doesn't know. As layers of ugly truth are peeled back and dark secrets are revealed, the duo find themselves in a struggle for survival when they unravel a mystery that pits them against the most dangerous forces in their lives.

A contemporary southern gothic thriller with frightening supernatural overtones, Alan Baxter's *Manifest Recall* explores the tragic life of a hitman who finds himself on the wrong side of his criminal syndicate. Baxter's adrenaline-fueled approach to storytelling draws readers into Eli Carver's downward spiral of psychosis and through the darkest realms of lost memories, human guilt and the insurmountable quest for personal redemption.

"If you like crime/noir horror hybrids, check out Alan Baxter's *Manifest Recall*. It's a fast, gritty, mind-f*ck." — Paul Tremblay, Bram Stoker Award-winning author of *A Head Full of Ghosts*

"Alan Baxter's fiction is dark, disturbing, hard-hitting and heart-breakingly honest. He reflects on worlds known and unknown with compassion, and demonstrates an almost second-sight into human behaviour." — Kaaron Warren, Shirley Jackson Award-winning author of *The Grief Hole*

"Alan Baxter is an accomplished storyteller who ably evokes magic and menace." — Laird Barron, author of *Swift to Chase*

GREY MATTER
P R E S S

greymatterpress.com

"A POWERFUL TALE OF CRIME AND DEATH,
CLEVERLY CRAFTED AND FLAWLESSLY EXECUTED."
JAMES A. MOORE, AUTHOR OF SEVEN FORGES

DEVOURING DARK

ALAN BAXTER

DEVOURING DARK
BY ALAN BAXTER

Matt McLeod is a man plagued since childhood by a malevolent darkness that threatens to consume him. Following a lifetime spent wrestling for control over this lethal onslaught, he's learned to wield his mysterious paranormal skill to achieve an odious goal: retribution as a supernatural vigilante.

When one such hit goes bad, McLeod finds himself ensnared in a multi-tentacled criminal enterprise caught between a corrupt cop and a brutal mobster. His only promise of salvation may be a bewitching young woman who shares his dark talent but has murderous designs of her own.

Devouring Dark is a genre-smashing supernatural thriller that masterfully blends elements of crime and horror in an adrenaline-fueled, life-or-death rollercoaster ride that's emblematic of the fiction from award-winning author Alan Baxter.

"*Devouring Dark* is a thrilling mix of crime and horror, a book that somehow defies either description yet embraces both. It moves like a juggernaut, thundering towards an intense, emotional conclusion. " — Gary McMahon, author of *Pretty Little Dead Things*

"*Devouring Dark* is a powerful tale of crime and death, cleverly crafted and flawlessly executed. I'm a fan of Alan Baxter and *Devouring Dark* is a perfect example of why." — James A. Moore, author of *Seven Forges* and the *Serenity Falls* Trilogy

"Action-packed yet emotionally resonant, Devouring Dark held me to the last page." — Kaaron Warren, Shirley Jackson Award-winning author of *Tide of Stone*

GREY MATTER
P R E S S

greymatterpress.com

AVAILABLE NOW
FROM GREY MATTER PRESS

Before — Paul Kane

The Bell Witch — John F.D. Taff

Dark Visions I — eds. Anthony Rivera & Sharon Lawson

Dark Visions II — eds. Anthony Rivera & Sharon Lawson

Death's Realm — eds. Anthony Rivera & Sharon Lawson

Devouring Dark — Alan Baxter

Dread — eds. Anthony Rivera & Sharon Lawson

The End in All Beginnings — John F.D. Taff

Equilibrium Overturned — eds. Anthony Rivera & Sharon Lawson

The Fearing: The Definitive Edition — John F.D. Taff

I Can Taste the Blood — eds. John F.D. Taff & Anthony Rivera

The Isle — John C. Foster

Kill-Off — John F.D. Taff

Little Black Spots — John F.D. Taff

Little Deaths: The Definitive Collection — John F.D. Taff

Manifest Recall — Alan Baxter

Mister White: A Dark Thriller — John C. Foster

Ominous Realities — eds. Anthony Rivera & Sharon Lawson

Peel Back the Skin — eds. Anthony Rivera & Sharon Lawson

Recall Night — Alan Baxter

Savage Beasts — eds. Anthony Rivera & Sharon Lawson

Secrets of the Weird — Chad Stroup

Seeing Double — Karen Runge

Served Cold — Alan Baxter

Splatterlands — eds. Anthony Rivera & Sharon Lawson

Suspended in Dusk II: Anthology of Horror — ed. Simon Dewar

Printed in Great Britain
by Amazon

22165329R00119